# THE
# YAGE
# LETTERS
*Redux*

# THE
# YAGE
# LETTERS
## *Redux*

William Burroughs
&
Allen Ginsberg

---

Edited and with an Introduction
by
Oliver Harris

CITY LIGHTS BOOKS
San Francisco

10 9 8 7

Cover design: Ella Harris
Text design and composition: Harvest Graphics
Editor: Robert Sharrard

The cover photograph of a *curandero* from the Vaupés region of Colombia is
reprinted by permission of the Botanical Museum of Harvard University.
The authors' thanks must be given to Alene Lee who in 1953 helped type
"In Search of Yage" and to Melville Hardiment who preserved Ginsberg's
1960 letter.

Before the first edition of *The Yage Letters* was published (in November
1963), six of the "In Search of Yage" letters had appeared in *Big Table* No. 2
(Summer 1959), five in *Kulchur* No. 3 (1961), and one in *Black Mountain
Review* No. 7 (Spring 1958) — although that letter ( July 10, 1953) was not
included in *The Yage Letters* until the second edition ( June 1975). Burroughs'
1960 letter was in *Floating Bear* No. 5 (1961) and his text, "I Am Dying,
Meester?" in *City Lights Journal* No. 1 (1963). "Roosevelt After Inauguration,"
which was included in *The Yage Letters* from the third edition (February 1988),
was first published in *Floating Bear* No. 9 (1961).

A Cataloging-in-Publication record has been established for this book by
the Library of Congress.
        ISBN-10: 0-87286-448-0
        ISBN-13: 978-0-87286-448-1

www.citylights.com

CITY LIGHTS BOOKS are edited by Lawrence Ferlinghetti and Nancy J.
Peters and published at the City Lights Bookstore, 261 Columbus Avenue,
San Francisco, CA 94133.

# Contents

# Acknowledgements

It is a great pleasure to be able to thank the following people for their assistance and support: for sharing their personal knowledge of the history of Burroughs' manuscripts, Alan Ansen, Lawrence Ferlinghetti, and Robert Creeley; for advice on the Ginsberg material, Barry Miles, and for his expert help in editing it, Bill Morgan; for helping with ayahuasca research, Wade Davis, Dennis McKenna, Luis Eduardo Luna, Arno Adelaars, Frederick Bois-Mariage, Terry Wilson, James Musser, John Allen and Tango; for help researching Burroughs' travels in 1953 with the Cacao Expedition, David Butler (Cocoa Research Unit, University of West Indies), Chris Turnbull (International Cocoa Germplasm Database, University of Reading), Basil Bartley and, especially, Paul Holliday.

My thanks also to James Grauerholz for practical support and research expertise, to Bob Rosenthal of the Allen Ginsberg Trust for generous permissions to publish, to Stefan Gutermuth for perfecting the cover design, and to Robert Sharrard for his patience as an editor.

For permissions to publish material and for their personal assistance, I want to thank Bernard Crystal (Rare Books and Manuscripts, Butler Library, Columbia University, New York); Anthony Bliss (Rare Books and Literary Manuscripts, The Bancroft Library, University of California, Berkeley); Richard Clement (Kenneth Spencer Research Library,

University of Kansas). For permissions to publish and for archival assistance, I want to thank Becky Cape and Anthony Tedeschi (Lilly Library, Indiana University); William McPheron, Sean Quimby, Roberto Trujillo, and L. Scott (Department of Special Collections, Green Library, Stanford University); Petrina Jackson (Rare and Manuscript Collections, Kroch Library, Cornell University); and Sandra Roscoe and Jessica Westphal (Special Collections Research Centre, University of Chicago Library).

I want to thank the Arts and Humanities Research Board for the Research Leave Scheme award, and Keele University for the sabbatical leave, that allowed me to complete the work. Thanks also to Keith Seward, Jim McClaverty, Rajmil Fischman, Andy Dobson, Ian MacFadyen, and to all my family.

Finally, I would like to dedicate *The Yage Letters Redux* to Lawrence Ferlinghetti, who made possible the first edition in 1963, and to the late Robert Creeley, who had the foresight to publish the first part of it back in 1957; as he would have put it, "Onward!"

# Introduction

## "PART OF THE MYSTERY"

I remember coming across *The Yage Letters* for the first time in a little New Age bookshop in Oxford some time around 1980. Hidden on a shelf in between works of ethnography and guides to astral travel, there it was, this very small, very slim City Lights paperback. On its cover of unbelievably black, inky darkness, the ghostly image of an Indian shaman floated, like a figure from some lost, archaic world. I was immediately captivated — if also stumped by the mysterious title I didn't know how to pronounce and by the thought that this was an "epistolary novel," as it said on the back cover. Was this a work of anthropology, non-fiction letters, literature? A quarter of a century later, having had the experience of editing Burroughs' letters and his first novel, I ought to know. But for all the mysteries that can be explained away, *The Yage Letters* remains decidedly anomalous and enigmatic, as befits a book made up of unresolved quests to discover an elusive Grail.

Since it was first published in 1963, *The Yage Letters* has changed and grown larger through two revised editions in 1975 and 1988, and that original book, so svelte it could fit in your hip pocket, now has the aura of a lost object from the past. But texts don't remain fixed, frozen in time, and there are gains as well as losses in the process of revision. This new, expanded *Yage Letters Redux* won't have the last word, but it will be the first to re-edit the text by going back into its manuscript and publishing histories and so to uncover stories untold for forty years.

It's no coincidence that most of what has been written about the book —and relatively little has been—focuses on just "In Search of Yage," the first of its three parts. True, the narrative presented as a dozen letters from Burroughs to Ginsberg between January and July 1953 is by far the longest part, and the most important. But overlooking "Seven Years Later"—the exchange of letters between the two men in June 1960—and "Epilogue"—Ginsberg's note from 1963 and Burroughs' cut-up text, "I Am Dying, Meester?"—is also a way to keep it simple. How else to make sense of this strange hybrid produced by two writers, across two decades?

This is the mystery of the text itself, and telling for the first time the story of how its individual parts were written and collected together is one aim of this Introduction. The other is to show that beyond the mythology of *The Yage Letters* as an exotic search for fabled drugs in tropical jungles there lies a significant and equally interesting historical reality. Together, these two narratives reveal the rich complexity of *The Yage Letters* that belies its appearance as only a minor, eccentric work.

With writing in it from both the 1950s and '60s, *The Yage Letters* has a unique place within the trajectory of the Burroughs oeuvre, within the biographies of both Burroughs and Ginsberg, and within the cultural history of the Beat movement. No book is better suited to mark the fiftieth anniversary of City Lights as an independent publisher of the unorthodox and alternative. Of course, Lawrence Ferlinghetti was also the long-time publisher of Ginsberg, who made two vital contributions to *The Yage Letters* — not only his 1960 letter, an extraordinarily intense outpouring of drug-fueled psychic and spiritual anguish, but also his struggle to get Burroughs' book into print. This decade-long labour on Burroughs' behalf is what makes it also Ginsberg's book; such is the strange, composite authorship of *The Yage Letters*.

It is, too, a work of equally intriguing genre confusion, even its first part being a hybrid of the comic picaresque tradition, travel writing, the ethnobotanical field report, political satire, psychedelic literature, and epistolary narrative. It reads at times like *A Yaqui Way of Knowledge* by Carlos Castaneda—who was half way through apprenticing himself to Don Juan the year *The Yage Letters* was published — and at other times like Che Guevara's *Motorcycle Diaries* — reporting on the same region just a year before Burroughs' travels — as if rewritten in Louis-Ferdinand Céline's style of bitter comedy in *Journey to the End of the Night*. And what of the specific object of its quest? Described as "*la maravillosa planta*" or "weirdest of the hallucinogens," the Amazonian drug is the mystery wrapped within the mystery of the text.

The history of the "vine of the soul" can wait, but its very name poses an immediate conundrum. Burroughs wrote the word "Yage," as if it rhymed with "age"; but it is properly written "*yagé*" and pronounced (as Burroughs knew) "ya-hey." Why not simply correct the spelling? After all, the error gives the impression of a kind of willed ignorance, less a personal idiosyncrasy than a mistranslation that disrespects the language of the drug's indigenous culture—in effect, an act of colonial appropriation. And yet to fix the problem now and change the book's very title would be to resolve a lack of fixity, an ambiguous duplicity that has always been a part of the text and readers' experience of it. Because of this ongoing confusion, rather than despite it, I reserve "Yage" for *The Yage Letters* and use "*yagé*" in all other contexts. This fits my aim to respect the historical text, but it was an awkward decision and I was relieved when a fellow-editor confirmed my sense that it's the appropriate one: "I think you should stick with your argument about the title. As an ignorant reader (I wasn't sure how to pronounce it), it's part of the mystery."[1]

## "I'M THE MAN WHO CAN DIG IT"

Jack Kerouac's journeys on the American road made travel central to Beat writing, but of the three major figures the real travel writers were Burroughs and Ginsberg. They journeyed further and for longer, nomads geographically and imaginatively, because each knew they were internal exiles — aliens in their own land, even in their own bodies. In late 1949 Burroughs escaped the States and relocated his family from Texas to Mexico City, so beginning twenty-five years as a writer-in-exile.

Demonized as an addict and homosexual, Burroughs simply could not have written his first two titles, *Junkie*[2] and *Queer*, inside the disciplinary straitjacket of Cold War America. And so he moved south through the Americas half in flight and half in quest, trying to outrun his addict identity as documented in *Junkie* and the fixations of desire as narrated in *Queer*. His first novel ended famously with the promise of a new Grail — "Yage may be the final fix" — although this line was actually added to anticipate *Queer*, its intended sequel, which described the unsuccessful two-month trip through Panama and Ecuador he made in July and August 1951 with Lewis Marker (the Allerton of *Queer*). It's easily missed, but the second line of "In Search of Yage" — which speaks of going "back among the Indians"—links his seven-month expedition in 1953 to that first trip. But what was Burroughs doing in the Amazon, and why was *yagé* the object of his quest? What persuaded him to trade his snap-brim fedora for a pith helmet?

Increasingly disillusioned with Mexico, in Spring 1951 Burroughs told Kerouac that, for "business" reasons, he was "ready to shove — South."[3] That Christmas—now in the wake of the disastrous shooting of his wife, Joan — he asked Ginsberg if he and Kerouac would "consider Ecuador." Eager to exploit its economic and social "frontier" conditions, Burroughs was hoping to settle down there. This was the start of an obsession with the continent, apparent in letters throughout the decade that spoke of plans to return to the site of his "real destiny." The earliest references to *yagé* itself don't appear in his correspondence until early March 1952, and then only in the negative. He filled Ginsberg in on his trip to Ecuador: "Did not score for Yage, Bannisteria caapi, Telepathine, Ayahuasca — all names for the same drug. I think the deal is top secret. I know the Russians are working on it, and I think U.S. also." Burroughs' interest was only increased by the enigmatic report he received from Dr. Lewis Wolberg, one of his former psychiatrists — " 'There seems to be some mystery about this drug,' he wrote me"— and two months later, in May 1952, his mind was made up: "No doubt about it. Yage is a deal of tremendous implications, and I'm the man who can dig it."

As for Burroughs' *qualifications*, in a sense he had been preparing for an expedition since his graduate studies in anthropology at Harvard in 1938 and, later, at Columbia. Then again, while Burroughs had also taken anthropology, archaeology, and ethnology classes at Mexico City College during 1950, he had never received any training in botany or plant chemistry nor ever made a field trip — and he would be heading into remote, virgin jungle to search out a drug almost unknown to Western science.

However, it's not only a matter of Burroughs' *scientific* credentials, and there is a trace of hysteria in his claim to be "the man who can dig it." By late May 1952, the psychological element was on the surface: "*I must go*," he now told Ginsberg, "*I must find the Yage*." The sense of compulsion suggests that Burroughs' quest for a drug rumoured to have visionary healing powers had equally to do with its tremendous implications for *internal* secrets and mysteries. As he concluded: "For some reason I have forebodings about this S.A. expedition. Don't know why except it seems a sort of final attempt to 'change fact.' Well, *a ver* (we shall see)." What underlay his angst—the distress of his failed relationship with Marker, the trauma of killing his wife, of losing his children, of staring into an uncertain future — this, too, qualified Burroughs as the "man who can dig" a magic drug that promised to "change fact."

But mysteries remain about precisely what he knew and what he found. Was Burroughs just a clueless amateur, stumbling through the jungle "comically underprepared," as James Campbell puts it?[4] And if not, then what is the place of *The Yage Letters* in general and "In Search of Yage" in particular within the history of Amazonian ethnobotany and travel writing?

## "IT IS STILL AN ENIGMA"

The first mystery concerns the elusive source of Burroughs' information. Ginsberg later suspected that "he'd read about [it] probably in some crime magazine or *National Geographic* or *New York Enquirer* or some goofy tabloid newspaper."[5] But in 1951 there couldn't have been much information in the popular press because there was very little even in the scientific literature. At that time, whatever source Burroughs found was a discovery in itself.

In fact, *yagé*— or *ayahuasca* (pronounced "EYE-a-wasca"), as both the vine and the psychoactive drinks made from it are now more commonly known—had only been discovered for Western science exactly one hundred years earlier, in 1851, by the great Victorian naturalist Richard Spruce, whose *Notes of a Botanist on the Amazon and Andes* (published in 1908) Burroughs knew. After that, there were few important scientific advances until the early 1920s, when the work of South American botanists and pharmacists was complemented by European researchers, including the German pharmacologist Louis Lewin, whose classic study, *Phantasica*, Burroughs probably read at Harvard. But there was no breakthrough that might have caught the non-specialist's eye for another thirty years, when the inheritor of Spruce's mantle, the "father of ethnobotany" who oversaw the birth of "ethnopsychopharmacology,"[6] the legendary Richard Evans Schultes (1915-2001), started to publish on the subject. Describing it in 1963 as one of "the weirdest of our phantastica or hallucinogens," Schultes (pronounced "SHULL-tees"), observed that ayahuasca "remains one of the most poorly understood American narcotics today."[7]

Nowadays, a wealth of information is available to anyone with access to the Internet, which has massively spread public awareness of a drug already popularised by celebrity users — creating a problem with "ayahuasca tourism" in the region — and by high profile stories in the media. There are ongoing legal disputes with the United States about claims to patent the drug for pharmaceutical exploitation and to ban even its sacramental use (by the Brazilian *Santo Daime* and the *União de Vegetal* Churches and other cults) — key battles in a broader effort to control the right to visionary experience. The sheer number of books about ayahuasca published in recent years makes it hard to grasp just how obscure the drug was half a century ago, or to recognise the sudden cultural shift that took place a decade later with the dawn of the psychedelic 1960s.

The ten-year delay in publication was therefore an ironic key to the book's reception. Back in May 1953, Burroughs had anticipated the effects of a possible article in *Life* magazine (by the "*Encounter*" reporter of "In Search of Yage"): "The U.S. will be Yage conscious for sure when that issue hits the stands." On the contrary, in 1953 there was no "free publicity," as he put it, to exploit. It wouldn't be until May 1957 that an article in *Life* — Gordon Wasson's "Seeking the Magic Mushrooms" — started to create public interest in natural hallucinogens. In 1963, Burroughs' work appeared at exactly the right moment, and was effectively advertised in advance that June by the debut issue of *The Psychedelic Review*, which included writings on sacred mushroom use by Wasson and on LSD by Gerald Heard, and whose editorial actually named Burroughs as the latest in the tradition of drug-using literary visionaries.

In the larger picture, 1963 was also the year that City Lights published *Miserable Miracle*, the translation of Henri Michaux's experiences of mescaline, that Timothy Leary and Richard Alpert were sacked by Harvard for their LSD experiments, and that Aldous Huxley died (in the last week of November, as Burroughs' book rolled off the presses). Six months later, Ken Kesey and his Merry Pranksters took their bus on the road, launching their Acid Tests and announcing the arrival of the psychedelic youth counterculture. Of course, this was no unified movement: Burroughs didn't get on with Leary (any more than Schultes did), dashing Ginsberg's optimism that "Bill & Leary at Harvard are going to start a beautiful consciousness alteration of the whole world."[8] In fact, with his typically prescient paranoia (motivated by bad trips on LSD and DMT), Burroughs cautioned against psychedelics: *"They are poisoning and monopolizing the hallucinogen drugs,"* he warns in *Nova Express* (1964). Nevertheless, there "can be little doubt," observed Schultes, "that the second half of the twentieth century will be remembered as a time when 'mind-altering,' or hallucinogenic, substances came into increasing use, serious as well as frivolous, in sophisticated Western societies."[9] In 1963 the U.S. was ready to be *yagé* conscious, and Ralph Metzner rightly observes that the "shamanic lore of ayahuasca entered most strongly into Western culture initially through *The Yage Letters*."[10] Then again, as Schultes and Metzner acknowledge, what was new in the West had been sacred and medicinal custom for millennia in the New World tropics.

It was an unlikely coincidence that in 1953 Burroughs and Schultes should have met in Colombia, a chance convergence of two Harvard men embarked on very different careers. Their encounter has been often noted, but only observed in any detail by Wade Davis in his biography of Schultes, *One River* (1996), and his beautiful "photographic journey," *The Lost Amazon* (2004). One thing that has gone unnoticed is the material evidence that links the most famous picture of Burroughs — standing in the jungle outside Mocoa, holding his pith helmet in one hand, the other gripping an ayahuasca vine, gazing to his right — and a picture in Schultes' *Vine of the Soul* of one of his Indian assistants against the same background, looking left: they're two halves of the same scene, confirming it was Schultes himself who took the picture of Burroughs with his twin-lens Rolleiflex.[11] But what the men made of each other is still mostly speculation, and Burroughs' portrait of "Doc Schindler" is curiously inconsistent — note how he brazenly ventriloquizes the softly-spoken Boston Brahmin in Lee's own rogue's voice ("Bill, I haven't been fifteen years in this sonofabitch country and lost all my teeth in the service without picking up a few angles").

In practice, meeting Schultes — who in 1953 was completing 12 years of almost continuous fieldwork in the Northwest Amazon — was a turning point in Burroughs' explorations. In January and February, he had made a five-week round-trip on his own from Bogotá to Puerto Asís, during which his observations of the Colombian Civil War were more significant than the *yagé* he took in Puerto Límon (the very place where, in 1942, Schultes had first taken it). Then in March Burroughs traveled with Schultes, who had teamed up with the Anglo-Colombian Cacao Expedition (the "Cocoa Commission"), for part of a second, thousand-mile round-trip from Bogotá to Puerto Leguizamo. Outside Mocoa Burroughs first experiences the force of *yagé*, and his description of the set and setting features all the key stages, from *la purga* (the wracking, purgative nausea) through *la chuma* or *mareación* (dizzying intoxication) to *la pinta* (the visions). The itinerary of "In Search of Yage" and Burroughs' other letters from this period give a more or less accurate record, but only another point of view could confirm details and complete the picture, and Schultes was never forthcoming. The botanical diaries of Paul Holliday, one member of the Cacao Expedition exploring the region for witches' broom disease, therefore provide a unique account, including on-the-spot descriptions of their first encounter and Burroughs' *yagé* trip near Mocoa:

10/3/53: Stayed at Hotel Niza in Pasto. We found Burroughs, an American, with a publishing firm, commissioned to write a book about narcotics in the Putumayo, having come by road from Cali. A tall, lank, droopy sort of person with a pessimistic streak for conjuring up all manner of fearful fevers one can collect around Putumayo; a pleasant fellow though, talkative and dryly amusing.

19/3/53: Burroughs has just about recovered from his yahé drinking. The old Ingano Indian gave him a wineglass full of the stuff (a mixture of two alkaloids from a wild plant), and within 15 min. it sent him almost completely off his rocker: violent vomiting every few minutes, feet almost numb & hands almost useless, unable to walk straight, liable to do anything one would not dream of doing in a normal state [. . .] He got back to the hotel [Hotel America, Mocoa] about seven this morning after a pretty awful night.

Other details confirm the impression that Burroughs earned respect for sheer physical boldness, but was not taken seriously by either the British botanists or Schultes. This picture is hardly contradicted by "In Search of Yage," which is far more about the misadventures of searching than the finding, or by the rest of *The Yage Letters*, where Burroughs' apparent knowledge is eclipsed by Ginsberg's much shorter but more focused account. Appearances, however, could not be more deceptive.

Ginsberg's 1960 letter is, like the copious journals he kept throughout his Latin American trip, loquacious and introspective, both poetic about the drug—"visit the moon, see the dead, see God"—and explicit about its shattering effects on his ego — "I'm no Curandero, I'm lost myself." Seeking out ayahuasca was more than a continuation of Ginsberg's other creative experiments with hallucinogens—mescaline, nitrous oxide, LSD and psilocybin mushrooms—although it did result in at least one important poem, "Magic Psalm." Rather, the main reason he followed in Burroughs' footsteps and made his own seven-month trip (originally, he had traveled with Ferlinghetti to a conference in Chile, and planned to stay just one month) was anxiety about what his status as the world's most famous poet was doing to his self-image. That is why, terrified by the visions of ego-death that overwhelmed him, Ginsberg appealed to his old Master for help. Needless to say, he wasn't ready for Burroughs' enigmatic reply. Ginsberg didn't understand the advice to use his new cut-up method as a way to complete the drug's "derangement of the senses" (the phrase of Rimbaud's that Burroughs used to describe both *yagé* intoxication *and* the cut-ups' goal of deconstructing the illusion of reality): "I thought he should have held my hand more," Ginsberg said in an interview years later, "instead of telling me there was no hand to hold."[12] The irony here is that Burroughs seems to be "the knowing one," as Ginsberg's interviewer puts it, when on the evidence of the text Ginsberg had had the more profound encounter with *yagé*.

From a specifically ethnobotanical point of view, Ginsberg's writing also marks a crucial difference in knowledge. For he describes accurately the single most important element that distinguishes ayahuasca from all other natural hallucinogens — namely the potency that derives from a unique synergy of pharmacological substances taken in combination. Of the many additives used, two are of outstanding importance: one, *chagropanga*, had been identified as *Diplopterys cabrerana,* another vine of the *Banisteriopsis* family, and the other, an evergreen shrub known as *chacruna*, whose precise botanical identity remained in the 1950s a mystery. In Schultes' own account:

Both of these plants have in their leaves a different hallucinogenic chemical — tryptamine — from the active principles — beta-carbolines — found in Banisteriopsis. Addition of these leaves greatly enhances and lengthens the intoxication through a kind of synergistic activity. How, one wonders, did these Indians find from the 80,000 species around them these two additives with such extraordinary effects?[13]

This achievement of shamanic alchemy only began to be understood scientifically in the 1960s, when it was recognized that the consciousness-expanding effects of ayahuasca brews result from the presence of the mildly psychotropic β-carboline alkaloids in the vine (harmine and harmaline), which function as an MAO (monoamine oxidase) inhibiter, which is what activates the otherwise orally inert psychedelic agent, DMT (dimethyltryptamine). Writing in the mid-1980s, Schultes concluded of this ancient and remarkable nexus of botany and chemistry: "It is still an enigma."[14]

Pharmacologically, this synergy is the real story of ayahuasca, and Ginsberg gives an early glimpse of it in his 1960 letter from Pucallpa, where he reports that the curandero gave him a "mix" including "a catalyst known as the 'Mescla'" which "in Pucallpa is called Chacruna." Although Ginsberg adds that "the preparation is not excessively secret — I think Schultes saw and knows," in fact the botanical identity of *chacruna* and its function was precisely the secret Burroughs appeared not to know.

However, seven years earlier Burroughs had in fact made the discovery of *chacruna* and immediately recognized its significance. Also in Pucallpa, now half-way through his third and longest trip through Peru, he dashed off his letter to Ginsberg in urgent, hasty pencil on June 18:

Hold the presses! Everything I wrote about Yage subject to revision in the light of subsequent experience. It is *not* like weed, nor anything else I have ever experienced. I am now prepared to believe the *Brujos* do have secrets, and that Yage alone is quite different from Yage prepared with the leaves and plants the *Brujos* add to it.

Burroughs added a comment on his original "Yage" manuscript, noting that these leaves were "*essential* for full hallucinating effect" and also that he had "identified [the plant] as *Palicourea Sp. Rubiaceae*" (see Appendix 1). Quite how he made this identification is itself a mystery, but from his "*Yagé* Article" written two years later it's clear he knew the medicine man, named Saboya, had let him in on "a trade secret" (see Appendix 5). It turns out that in June 1953 Burroughs was making the most accurate classification to date—"Indeed, the first real botanical achievement in the scientific appraisal of ayahuasca since Spruce's seminal work in the 1850s"[15] — since he was the first to identify the genus of the plant now more correctly classified as *Psychotria viridis*. We're left, therefore, with one final mystery: why Burroughs' discovery, worthy of a place in ethnobotanical history, was left out of "In Search of Yage"—why he did not "hold the presses."

There are two likely answers. The first is the contingency of the manuscript history of what became "In Search of Yage" (as revealed in the following sections); in other words, it wasn't necessarily deliberate. Burroughs was certainly aware of his contribution to botany, telling Ginsberg in January 1955 of his disappointment that Schultes had stopped corresponding with him, bearing in mind he had "sent a specimen of the plant used to potentiate Yage that I collected in Peru (hitherto, the other ingredients *were not known*, so it is a matter of some importance)."[16] The other reason is hinted at in Burroughs' June 18 letter, when he speaks of admitting that the *Brujos* "do have secrets." For Burroughs took the empirical approach of a skeptical Westerner, and this inclined him to resist indigenous knowledge — clearest in "In Search of Yage" when he rails that "the most inveterate drunk, liar and loafer in the village is invariably the medicine man." Of course, this is William *Lee*'s cynicism, and Burroughs himself not only revised his opinion of medicine men but, in the Pucallpa notes section of his July 8 letter, announced that he had indeed found the Grail, momentously declaring: "Yage is it."

In short, Burroughs seems to answer the question posed forty years ago by Donatella Manganotti: "Was Yage the *real* thing, the 'final fix' and as such too important to be told in so many words — like esoteric mysteries of the past?"[17] In his "*Yagé* Article" Burroughs claimed the drug showed him "a new state of being"— a spur to his belief in the "Magical Universe" and, later, in Castaneda's world of the *nagual* — that called for a total reevaluation of knowledge of the world:

> I must give up the attempt to explain, to seek any answer in terms of cause and effect and prediction, leave behind the entire structure of pragmatic, result seeking, use seeking, question asking Western thought. I must change my whole method of conceiving fact.

But the context of Burroughs' revelation is as important as the content. Here, in his "*Yagé* Article," motivated as a serious enquiry, he could without ambiguity make such claims. In the mouth of William Lee, he could not — until his final letter. Which brings us to the literary identity of "In Search of Yage" and the politics of its travel writer.

## "THE CALL OF THE SECRET"

Burroughs' Pucallpa visions led on to Lee's final destination, the Composite City, where *yagé* is dramatically defined as "space time travel." This in turn became Burroughs' definition of *writing*, and the rest of his oeuvre is governed by this understanding. It's therefore essential to recognise the particular textuality of this extraordinary drug-inspired vision. In this phantasmagoric scene, meeting point of "the unknown past and the emergent future," the experience of traveling in space and time is not only described but actually *produced* for the reader, who encounters a collage of phrases and images taken from the preceding letters. Creating uncanny flashbacks, this literally composite text is a special kind of "travel writing," and an augury and precedent for the experimental practices of "I Am Dying, Meester?" the cut-up text from the next decade that ends *The Yage Letters*.

Rewriting the geographic reality of South America as an imaginative one, Burroughs here redefines himself as cartographer of the *unknown* — a key word in the Composite City vision — "a map maker, an explorer of psychic areas," as he would declare in 1962. Far from being marginal, his slight epistolary travelogue is of the essence for his future writing — his writing *of* the future.

The vision of the Composite City anticipates (and, minus the letter's opening lines of address, also appears in) *Naked Lunch*, whose radical novelty for Mary McCarthy was to make a montage out of "biochemistry, anthropology, and politics," and yet which, "with its extracts from a diary, like a ship's log, its pharmacopoeia, has the flavor of eighteenth-century satire."[18] Burroughs himself saw his adventures as belonging to the picaresque tradition. In this reading, Lee as a wastrel and an exile follows in the footsteps of Thomas Nashe's *The Unfortunate Traveller*, and there are precise as well as general resemblances to his Elizabethan forbear: Jack Wilton's refrain, "which of us all is not a sinner?" is echoed by Lee's "Who am I to talk?" to identify fellow-hustlers and champions of shamelessness. Lee's credentials as a picaro figure are set up in the first letter of "In Search of Yage," where he presents himself as a drug-taking queer sex tourist with a penchant for cynical and obscene fantasy. The very first line —"I stopped off here to have my piles out"—is a shock calculated to undercut any expectations of ethnographic "objectivity."

Equally, the picaresque matches Burroughs' affinity for the episodic, which in turn coincides with the minimally plotted structures of travel writing and the epistolary or journal form. In Burroughs, old and new forms are hyphenated and crossbred: for Terrence McKenna, his writing is "pharmo-picaresque"[19]—two kinds of trip in one. Indeed, in the early 1970s the McKenna brothers, Terrence and Dennis, were inspired by "In Search of Yage" to make their own search for mind-altering natural hallucinogens, writing it up as a mock-heroic mission "to chase the White Whale" along the Río Putumayo, having heard "The Call of the Secret."[20] In 2005, the travel writer Paul Theroux, recalling how *The Yage Letters* had "possessed" him — "I closed the book and thought: I really must repeat his trip"[21] — became the latest in a long line of those to follow Burroughs' example and answer the call.

## "WHAT WE NEED IS A NEW BOLIVAR"

"In Search of Yage" follows *Junkie*, which in 1951 Burroughs saw as "a travel book more than anything else," but which Alan Ansen more precisely described as an "anthropo-sociological travelogue."[22] The shift to foreign lands — mapping tropical jungles rather than mainly North American urban underworlds — not only connects travel writing more closely to its scientific double, ethnography, but to imperial adventure.[23] In the early 1950s, the American empire was massively expanding and interfering in Latin America through companies like United Fruit and under the guise of assistance programmes—note the reference to "Point Four and good nabor crap." Burroughs traveled through the region always aware of the exile's ironic power to still exercise the master race's privileges — his class identity projected here as the dark side of William Lee, the Ugly American.

This imperial identity is projected even more devastatingly in *Queer*, where Lee's interest in *yagé*—a major part of the narrative—is completely different to "In Search of Yage." Here, as in *Junkie*, the drug's telepathic power is politicized and militarized by invoking a Cold War context, which recalls Burroughs' claim in 1952 that "the Russians are working on it." This was paranoia grounded in historical reality: Burroughs' recollection that the Russians "were there in 1927 and took away a ton of *yagé*— I heard that everywhere,"[24] helps identify Varanof and Juzepczuk, who carried out fieldwork in the Colombian Caquetá in 1925-26. Fast-forward to April 13, 1953. Burroughs was back in Bogotá after his trip with Schultes, having been rescued from Villavicencio — "the hottest spot in all Colombia"— in Schultes' official Point Four car. On the same day in Washington, CIA Director Allen Dulles was authorising another government programme, this one top secret: MK-ULTRA. Designed to consolidate the development of mind-control drugs, the programme confirms Burroughs' prescience about plans to poison and monopolize the hallucinogen drugs. That Burroughs had once tried to enlist in the OSS, wartime forerunner of the CIA, was one of his more sinister qualifications as the man who could dig it.

The report on *yagé* he had received from Dr. Wolberg in May 1952 had prompted Burroughs to imagine "armies of telepathy-controlled zombies marching around"—a startling premonition of the race to perfect the Manchurian Candidate. The scenario of Richard Condon's novel, set in 1952 during the Korean War, precisely describes the kind of fears that drove the MK-ULTRA programme, and the CIA sponsored botanical research into obscure Amazonian vines to find brainwashing weapons of their own. This Cold War scenario had another South American connection, however, one that appears in "In Search of Yage" via its intersection with the Colombian Civil War.

Passing through Tolima in January, Burroughs describes an unpleasant, American-loving "nacional law who had fought in Korea." Although the detail is lost in Burroughs' general antipathy towards what he calls "the Palace Guard" of the Conservative Party, the fact of his fighting in Korea is far from incidental. For the neo-fascist Lauréano Gómez, who came to power in 1950, exploited the anti-communist climate set by Washington to justify internal political repression while serving America's national interests abroad. Indeed, as Mario Murillo observes in his recent history, "Gómez was the only Latin American leader who supported the U.S. war effort in Korea by actually sending Colombian forces to the region."[25] The Korean War veteran suddenly appears in a geopolitical context. In the twenty-first century, the alliance between George W. Bush and Alvaro Vélez Uribe has perpetuated just this relationship between America and Colombia, as the "war on communism" was followed by first the "war on drugs" and now the "war on terror."

Burroughs was well aware of *La Violencia*, as the long period of bloody repression in post-war Colombia came to be known, and when he describes the "air of unresolved and insoluble tension about Mocoa, the agencies of control out in force to put down an uprising which does not occur," his account isn't so different to that of Che Guevara passing through Bogotá a year earlier: "There is more repression of individual freedom here than in any country we've been to," he writes his mother in July 1952. "The atmosphere is tense and it seems a revolution may be brewing."[26]

Che Guevara and William Burroughs make unlikely bedfellows, but a fraction less implausible when we turn from "In Search of Yage" to see how explicit his political sympathies could be in letters from this time, as when writing to Ginsberg on April 22 that "it is *impossible* to remain neutral": "Wouldn't surprise me if I end up with the Liberal guerillas." Especially from *The Soft Machine* (1961) to *Cities of the Red Night* (1981), Burroughs would imaginatively join up with such forces in a global struggle modeled on this South American conflict. But in "In Search of Yage" Burroughs qualified such open and unambiguous positions. The Lee who unites with the anti-colonial aspirations of Latin American peoples to say, "What we need is a new Bolivar who will really get the job done," is also the Lee who plays the imperialist Ugly American abroad, able to buy what and whoever he wants with his "Yankee dollar." Such contradictions give his writing its unsettling power.

Although similar things could be said about his travels through Panama, Ecuador, and Peru, it is when traveling through the Putumayo region of Colombia that Burroughs most fully updates a history of exploitation by foreign powers based on the strategic importance of the area's resources, going back to the sixteenth century and the Spanish Conquistadors' search for gold. Shortly before the Capuchin missionaries took over, there was the *cinchona* bark boom of the 1870s, driven by the British demand for quinine to treat malaria. This led to the massive rubber boom that began in the 1890s and lasted over two appalling decades. Sourly observing in "In Search of Yage" that "the whole Putumayo region is on the down grade," Burroughs notes that "the rubber business is shot." But he seems to miss the point entirely. For the decline that had set in with the rise of rubber plantations in the East Indies had, as Schultes understood, "redounded to the benefit of the Indians, since the extraction of rubber from the wild could not compete with plantation production, thus saving thousands of lives of Amazon natives who were freed from merciless exploitation when the forest industry all but died out."[27]

The next stage in the region's history of strategic exploitation involved resources below the jungle floor, and is ironically presaged by Lee being mistaken for "a representative of the Texas Oil Company travelling incognito." Quipping that the locals saw the return of Texas Oil as "the second coming of Christ" ("and about as unlikely," he added in his original letter), Burroughs again fails to envision that it would be more like the second coming of the Conquistadors. The Governor of Mocoa was, in fact, right about the pool of oil nearby — the basin is estimated to contain two billion barrels' worth — but when Texaco moved in only a few years after Burroughs left, so began the process of driving thousands of Ingá, Siona, and Kofán Indians out. Not only the Putumayo's tribes, but the very land would be devastated. Of course, Burroughs wasn't actually an agent of Texas Oil, but there is a precise irony to another misrecognition he reports in a letter: "One theory had me down as a representative of

Squibb [Pharmaceuticals]. They were about to have a Yage boom." Clearly, Burroughs' powers of prophecy had their limits: then again, who in 1953 could have foreseen the rise of "biopiracy" extended to the vine of the soul?

Burroughs played the Ugly American ambiguously, at times blind to its operation, at others holding the identity up for coruscating critique. Take the way he puts down ideologically-blinkered American attitudes towards local suspicion of Point Four aid: "Like the U.S. Pegler fans say, 'The trouble is Unions.' They would still say it spitting blood from radiation sickness." But only a couple of years earlier Burroughs had himself been one of those "fans," writing Kerouac in one letter, "Unions! That's the trouble, unions!" and to Ginsberg describing the right-wing Westbrook Pegler as the only columnist "who possesses a grain of integrity." Now critiquing a position he had recently trumpeted, here the text shows traces of the political education Burroughs received in South America.

But the point is not so much the biographical context, as the many differences between Burroughs' correspondence and the overlapping letters of "In Search of Yage." For while the epistolary form makes it impossible to avoid thinking about the circumstances of the writer, it also forces us to make assumptions about the nature of the writing. Whether the letters of "In Search of Yage" are authentic records or literary works, or whether we attribute them to some composite figure inhabiting the interzone between fact and fiction — a hybrid of William Burroughs and his persona, William Lee — changes how we read them. And behind the received version of how these letters were written, there lies another story altogether.

## "I HAVE WRITTEN NOTHING YET"

When it comes to the writing of "In Search of Yage," the standard account is given by Burroughs' biographer, Ted Morgan: "he wrote long letters while on his Yage expedition, letters that were the initial form of a possible book."[28] But this familiar story is wrong on both counts. Firstly, comparison of his real and fictional letters does not show "the limited extent of Burroughs' reworking"—the sense I had of it back in 1991 for my Introduction to *The Letters of William S. Burroughs, 1945–1959*. More significantly, and surprisingly, the very idea that "In Search of Yage" grew out of Burroughs' real letters doesn't stand up to close scholarly scrutiny backed up by new manuscript research.

The first time Burroughs mentions plans for a book — the "Yage account"—is in the middle of January 1953.[29] Then there's nothing until his letter of March 3 from Bogotá. Here he rails against Ace Books, who a year earlier had delayed publication of *Junkie* to see if *Queer* could be added onto it, and now threatened the same again with his new work. "I have written nothing yet. I can't write out in the bush," Burroughs explained. "Why can't they go ahead and publish *Junkie* as is and later issue an edition with Yage part added? I don't know yet whether Yage will be book in itself. Oh well I am just confusing the issue further." Confusing the issue, yes, but also revealing another. Bear in mind that the "March 3" letter comes *fifth* in "In Search of Yage," some six thousand words into the text. And yet on this date Burroughs told Ginsberg he had so far "written nothing." Clearly, it's more than a matter of what Burroughs left in or edited out of his real correspondence.

On April 30, now in Guayaquil, Burroughs updated Ginsberg on his progress, or rather continued lack of it: "So far no success writing any-thing on Yage. My info is incomplete or some essential impetus is lack-ing."[30] In fact, it's not until May 3 that Burroughs began — "started last night," he told Ginsberg the next day — and thought he could write "50-100 pages on the Yage deal."[31] Finally, after working on it in longhand throughout May in Lima, and revising downwards its length — "I think the section will come to about 30-50 pages" — he at last sends Ginsberg a typed manuscript of "about 20 pages" in early June, noting: "This is still in rough form subject to corrections and additions." Between June and August he sends along "notes as they are in note-book" or "notes for insertion" — and then the trail of correspondence evidence dries up, as Burroughs returned, via stopovers in Mexico City and Florida, to ren-dezvous with Ginsberg in New York the last week of August 1953.

What makes this record of Burroughs' writing progress so extraordi-nary? At no time during his entire trip, from January to July, does he ever refer to his material as *letters*. And the reason is that the twenty-two page first draft "Yage" manuscript he mailed Ginsberg in June 1953 was not epistolary, in either form or origin. Contrary to all assumptions, "In Search of Yage" did not start out as real letters or edited letters or any kind of letters at all.

To put it in terms of crude statistics: of this 9,500 word manuscript, which is a sort of first-person travelogue journal, only 320 words definitely came from real letters. And to put this into perspective, 85% of this man-uscript was used for "In Search of Yage" and made up 80% of its first six letters ("January 15" to "April 15"). These six "letters" (sic) in turn make up 75% of the whole section. As for the last six ("May 5" to "July 10"), assembled after the June manuscript, just over a thousand words — about a quarter — came from real letters, while about half came from "notes" from his travel diaries typed out into letters and meant for insertion.

Far from Burroughs' real letters being the "initial form of a possible book," the idea of an epistolary text seems never once to have occurred to him. The questions we're left with, then, are how, when, and why Burroughs turned his "Yage" travelogue into the epistolary "In Search of Yage."

Apart from the "March 3" letter—none of which appeared in his June manuscript — Burroughs fabricated its epistolary appearance by adding material such as the letter's formal tops and tails, by changing the tense to create an improvised effect of reporting live, and by cutting out tell-tale lines. While some letters were created only by adding the formal openings and endings (such as "January 25"), in other cases (such as "February 28") Burroughs adapted the first and last paragraphs of real letters to use as frames for material in his non-epistolary manuscript. Other letters were more complex composites of the original manuscript, inserted notebook entries, new material, and selections from multiple real letters.

Inevitably, there were slip-ups, signs that give the game away. For example, in the letter supposedly written on February 28 a new line promises to "relate events more or less chronologically," which might seem to cover the dream of "Lima which I had not seen at this time." But Lima isn't seen until May 5, more than *two months* after "this time." There are also brusque shifts in tone and style, as when the second letter cuts straight into descriptive reportage with no preamble at all, in sharp contrast to the comic fantasy that ends the first letter (the Billy Bradshinkel routine — itself the most anomalous part of the original manuscript, but important for motivating the quest as an escape from haunting memories of home, family, and desire).

Such slips and continuity errors are hidden in plain view, however, because we don't tend to expect narrative coherence from letters. Still, to accept the appearance of authenticity also means overlooking the fact that none of the twelve letters here are signed "William Burroughs" (mostly "Bill" or "William"), while three are signed "Lee." This equivocation between the real and the fictional contradicts the book's unambiguous presentation of "In Search of Yage" as genuine letters from Burroughs to Ginsberg. But it is also, bizarrely, faithful to that real correspondence — since Burroughs and his fictive persona did sometimes trade places. For example, while the "May 12" letter in "In Search of Yage" is signed "Bill," his real May 12 letter, handwritten on small sheets of hotel stationary and without any literary pretensions, signs off "Willy Lee." Although Burroughs' unique creative merger of letters and literature wouldn't happen until the following year in Tangier — when the routines of *Naked Lunch* evolved directly from his letters to Ginsberg — it's as if, without quite knowing it, Burroughs was already fictionalising his letter-writing in anticipation of turning his "Yage" manuscript into an epistolary text.

## "THE SOUTH AMERICAN BOOK MIGHT TURN INTO SOMETHING OF INTEREST"

Burroughs reached New York in late August 1953 and, after six years of conducting a friendship entirely by long-distance mail, he now moved into Ginsberg's East 7th Street apartment off Tompkins Square. The received version of what happened next is that they worked on "Queer" and "Yage," but the only detail ever given is that they were aided by the typing of Alan Ansen and Alene Lee. It seems likely that Alene Lee (Kerouac's mixed-race lover at the time — Mardou Fox in *The Subterraneans*) retyped "Queer" in October and then "Yage," although there's no hard evidence (only a beautiful photograph of her and Burroughs relaxing together, taken by Ginsberg and later captioned, "Alene typed up the collaged manuscripts").[32] As for Ansen, he recalls playing no role in it at all.[33] So only two things about "Yage" are certain: the manuscript Burroughs brought with him was in a very rough state, and by the time he left for Tangier, in late December, it had taken on epistolary form.

The most vivid evidence for the state of the manuscript before they worked on it comes in a letter Ginsberg wrote to Malcolm Cowley, the celebrated editor at Viking Press:

> Burroughs is finishing assembling of notes for a second book on 2 years travels in Jungles and end-of-road-Conradian despair in mudhut Bolivian towns. He went down there to experiment with native magic and drugs, kind of an Ahab-quest; however survived and is in NY for September, then leaving for Africa. Book is a kind of more intense, imagic [?] & personal (tho in ways much more "'disciplined" than Kerouac) than travel books, is illustrated (photos) — is kind of a self-invented journal form (though he's thinking of turning it into novel). Writing gets to a kind of laconism and compression so that in parts the description resembles the anthropological-eastern deep psychic intensity of St. J-Perse's poetry.[34]

What's immediately apparent is that, in his eagerness to convey to Cowley the distinctive quality of Burroughs' writing, Ginsberg breathlessly presents the manuscript in terms of a bewildering and self-contradictory array of literary genres. He describes it in terms of notes, quests, travel literature, photo-illustration, the journal form, a potential novel, poetry—just about every form, in fact, apart from the epistolary.

A week later, Cowley wrote Ginsberg a polite reply, concluding: "It sounds as if the South American book might turn into something of interest."[35] This was spot on: the peculiarly hybrid and anomalous manuscript Ginsberg described clearly had still to "turn into" something. Exactly three months later he reported back that it now had: "The MSS. of Wm. Burroughs that I wrote you about is finished & can be read if you wish to."[36] (Cowley demurred, and never did get to see it.) As for what happened in between time, two scenarios seem possible.

It may be the idea came from Ginsberg, who might well have seen the letter as an appropriate way to solve Burroughs' generic problems, using the form to give the text a naturally loose unity. In the other scenario, we have to bear in mind the context of fraught desire in which the two men worked on the manuscript. For Burroughs had been pressuring Ginsberg into an intense sexual affair, determined by his fantasy of a total bodily merger he called "schlupping" (ominously, the aim of Lee with respect to Allerton in the other manuscript they were working on). In *this* context, it's likely that Burroughs was the one who seized on the epistolary. Addressing his material directly to Ginsberg, achieving a sort of merger of textual bodies, would have been a way for Burroughs to fuse his writing with the object of his desire—a prelude to his situation in Tangier the following year.

Finally, what of the new, epistolary "Yage"? Although the only complete December manuscript was probably lost in late 1956, we know that the manuscript contained significantly more material than ever appeared in "In Search of Yage." There were at least a further three letters, each in different ways highly important. One long letter, dated "June 23/28" from Pucallpa, featured the stunning, visionary *yagé* trip partly described in Burroughs' real June 18 letter and the notes in his July 8 letter. Another, "July 20" from Mexico, was still longer and contained most of the material that would appear as "Mexico City Return," the Epilogue to *Queer*, in 1985. A third, shorter letter, "May 24" from Lima (see Appendix 3), again changes dramatically our understanding of the relation between Burroughs' two manuscripts. For this was addressed not to "Allen" but to "Jean"— that is, the Gene Allerton of *Queer*— so revealing, thirty years earlier, another entirely unexpected overlap. The upshot is to confirm the prospect of a very different-looking "In Search of Yage" to the one eventually published in *The Yage Letters*.

## "GOLDEN PRESSURE"

If the manuscript history of "In Search of Yage" during 1953 was unexpectedly complicated, piecing together its evolution over the next decade shows the road to publication was no less so. Burroughs' plans for it first appear in September 1954, prompted by Aldous Huxley's *The Doors of Perception:* "Since Huxley's book on Peyote seems to have attracted attention, perhaps we could do something with the Yage material," he suggests to Ginsberg.[37] Ginsberg must have encouraged Burroughs because, by the end of December, he was now thinking of two separate projects — "the S.A. letters," and "a short book just on Yage like Huxley's peyote book. Positively no school-boy smut."[38]

This second, more sober and scientific project — possibly driven by Burroughs' disappointment that Schultes had put him down — began to take shape in early 1955 as a "short book with photos," but by October it had shrunk to "an article on Yage" and remained unwritten. Then in January 1956 Burroughs sent a first draft to Ginsberg (see Appendix 4), and a month later a second draft of almost 10,000 words (see Appendix 5). Cannibalising exactly half of "In Search of Yage," the great interest of the "*Yagé* Article" lies only partly in its explicit claims to serious research. Equally interesting is how differently "In Search of Yage" now reads in light of it. It's as if the particular and self-contradictory qualities of "In Search of Yage"—both the feel of authentic immediacy *and* the literary resonance of symbolic details—only become fully visible in contrast to a version stripped of its epistolary form.

Burroughs had an outlet in mind for his "*Yagé* Article" ("an adventure true magazine like *Argosy*"), but there were no obvious prospects for the manuscript he called "Yage Quest." At this time Ginsberg wrote to Kerouac, reflecting on his mission as agent for the Beat writers in general and Burroughs in particular: "I know my projects seldom materialize but that's life, I keep trying. One will sooner or later. Junk [i.e., *Junkie*] did anyway."[39] His letter also refers to a brand-new publishing venture, "Crazy lights," which he had heard was "stillborn." Fortunately, Ginsberg's report of the demise of City Lights was premature; but still, with no publisher in sight for any of his manuscripts, it was logical that Burroughs would look to magazines for their piecemeal publication.

The first to appear was a single "Yage" letter, published under his pseudonym, William Lee, in the Autumn 1957 issue of *Black Mountain Review*, the influential poetry magazine of Charles Olson's experimental arts college. Although Ginsberg was collecting the material for its editor, the poet Robert Creeley, the choice of Burroughs' "July 10, 1953" letter was actually guided by Kerouac.[40] A sign of the confusing overlap between Burroughs' manuscripts, the Composite City vision was presented as "from Naked Lunch, Book III: In Search of Yage." The text is one of the essential seeds of *Naked Lunch*—but it was also the spectacular climax to "In Search of Yage." And yet, because it had been cannibalised for *Naked Lunch*, the first "Yage" letter to be published wouldn't actually take its place in *The Yage Letters* until the second edition of 1975.

In the meantime, starting early in 1957, Ginsberg began promoting Burroughs by putting what he referred to as "golden pressure" on Ferlinghetti.[41] And so in September he explained the importance of getting his work published in an American — and specifically a Beat — context: "What Burroughs needs is *something* of his published at least as a sampler & City Lights would be perfect place — to put it in context with my work & other."[42] Since most of the *Naked Lunch* materials were "pornographically unpublishable in US," it's not surprising that Ginsberg picked up on an earlier expression of interest: "You once mentioned possibility of Burroughs's So[uth] American letters section as a small City Lites prose book." Ferlinghetti wrote back diplomatically that he couldn't promise anything, and then, in June the following year, he suggested rewriting the draft of *Naked Lunch* he had just turned down—by expanding the Composite City section, which, he felt, was "at the heart of everything."[43] Even at this early stage, Ferlinghetti was drawn to the "Yage" material.

The next part of what became "In Search of Yage" was published in the Chicago magazine *Big Table*. The material, titled "In Quest of Yage," was a curiously fragmented selection, comprising the fourth, fifth, sixth, seventh, tenth and eleventh letters of "In Search of Yage," and was preceded by essays on Burroughs from Paul Bowles and Alan Ansen. Ansen's informed and insightful essay, specially commissioned by editor Paul Carroll, included a detailed description of "Yage"—although his account of the manuscript didn't match the material published in *Big Table* at all.

After *Naked Lunch* appeared in July 1959, Ginsberg still hoped to get "Queer" and "Yage" into print, but again nothing came of his plans to publish whole manuscripts. Instead, he helped place a selection of "Yage" letters in Lita Hornick's New York literary magazine, *Kulchur*. The letters that appeared in 1961 under the title "In Search of Yage" were the first, second, third, eighth and ninth in the sequence published two years later — again forming a confusingly broken narrative. Meanwhile, a note on the "May 23" letter directed the reader to another magazine and still another of the scattered parts of "In Search of Yage"; this time to the routine "Roosevelt After Inauguration" in the June 1961 issue of *The Floating Bear*. That October, LeRoi Jones and Diane di Prima, who produced this little mimeographed circular, found themselves under arrest because of the routine, charged with distributing obscene materials through the mail. Although both were cleared, Lawrence Ferlinghetti would have taken note.

Ginsberg's "golden pressure" at last paid off in summer 1962. Writing from Calcutta that June, he asked if Ferlinghetti had "thought again of printing Burroughs's collected So[uth] American letters — they're all available in *Big Table, Kulchur* & *Floating Bear*—It would make a nice small prose book & it's all there in print now."[44] Next month, Ferlinghetti consulted Paul Bowles, who agreed it "would make a fine book."[45] Finally, on July 26, he wrote to Burroughs and received a two-line reply: "Thanks for your letter—Yes I would be glad to have you publish the Yage letters."[46]

What does this behind-the-scenes narrative tell us about the City Lights publication? Firstly, it confirms Ginsberg's remarkably active role on Burroughs' behalf over an entire decade, never giving up on Ferlinghetti as the text's ideal publisher. Ginsberg's labours appear all the more remarkable in light of their intensely fraught relationship, first strained by Burroughs' unwelcome sexual fantasy in the mid-1950s and later by his cold distance (during the early '60s Burroughs virtually stopped writing to him). Secondly, it shows the chaotic and curiously discontinuous pre-history of "In Search of Yage," published by magazines in scattered fragments out of chronological sequence and presented in ways seemingly designed to baffle the reader. And finally, as Ginsberg's last letter implies — "it's all there in print now" — the text originally accepted for publication consisted *only* of the materials published in certain magazines. This is actually the key revelation: since the original manuscript had been lost, all Ferlinghetti could do was reproduce those letters as already edited and published, making a whole out of the sum of these parts. Which leaves us with how the rest of *The Yage Letters* — the Ginsberg and Burroughs letters from 1960 and Burroughs' cut-up text — came to be added to "In Search of Yage."

Between September and November 1962 Ferlinghetti collected together — with some difficulty — the various magazine publications, and then the following January he reached agreement with Burroughs on the removal of the "Roosevelt" routine (because of "difficulty with the customs") and the addition of "I Am Dying, Meester?"[47] In fact, "Roosevelt" would stay in right until the long galley stage, when the British distributors, fearing legal action, pressured the London-based printers, Villiers, to have it pulled. From exchanges between printer and publisher, it's clear that Ferlinghetti had held doubts about the piece ("you were not very happy about it yourself," wrote John Sankey of Villiers just before publication, "especially the name Roosevelt");[48] so he was pleased when Ed Sanders published the routine in February 1964, running it off with Ginsberg's help as a tiny Fuck You Press mimeo pamphlet. A decade later, when preparing the second edition of *The Yage Letters*, Ferlinghetti again omitted it, although this time his idea was to publish the routine himself; after several delays, *Roosevelt After Inauguration and Other Atrocities* came out in 1979. It lacked, however, the "short preface giving the publishing history of the piece" that, in 1975, Burroughs had felt the routine deserved.[49] Eventually, in 1988 (a decade after it had already appeared in Carl Weissner's German translation, *Auf der Suche nach Yage*), "Roosevelt After Inauguration" at long last made it into the third City Lights edition. It's worth adding to this brief attempt to do the text's history justice, that "Roosevelt" does indeed fit; insofar as this political satire — a flight of historical fantasy as scripted by Westbrook Pegler and acted out by an obscene version of the Marx Brothers — is one more anomalous piece in a larger whole, loosely connected by precise thematic and verbal crossovers.

As for the other elements of *The Yage Letters*, Burroughs sent "I Am Dying, Meester?" to Ferlinghetti in January 1963 to feature in the debut issue of his *City Lights Journal*. The cut-up text was specifically intended to expand and conclude the whole book, having been made by recycling fragments of "In Search of Yage": in this, it doesn't only echo the Composite City, but grounds Burroughs' new technique in that *yagé*-inspired montage to reveal significant experimental continuities across decades.

The final two major additions only came about by chance, because of a trip to Europe Ferlinghetti made that Spring. Before rendezvousing with

Burroughs in Paris, he met Melville Hardiment in London, and found he had the manuscript of Ginsberg's 1960 letter. "It was a real stroke of luck for me to fall onto this," he wrote to Hardiment from Paris in June, "since it is such a great letter & the 7-years-delayed YAGE ANSWER to Burroughs' Yage Letters & I am seeing Burroughs here about putting it in the book."[50] Reporting that "Bill thinks it's a good idea,"[51] he then wrote to Ginsberg in Kyoto (where he was staying with Gary Snyder), asking if he could use the letter and its drawings.[52] Ginsberg not only agreed but suggested including another letter, adding a further twist to the epistolary exchange: "He *answered* my Pucallpa letter (his answer was published in one of the issues of Floating Bear)—did you ever see that? That would be appropriate."[53]

Ferlinghetti approved, but he was so impressed by the unpublished Ginsberg letter ("which will make book a much greener scene"),[54] that he now had reservations about letting "I Am Dying, Meester?" conclude the book. Even though Burroughs stood his ground on this one, it's still striking to realise that his own June 1960 letter was only included because of Ginsberg's suggestion in response to Ferlinghetti's proposal to use Ginsberg's letter. This weird circularity in turn reflected the fact that Burroughs and Ginsberg had not written to each other directly—in relation to the epistolary text they were assembling, a bizarre irony — which meant Burroughs was often the last to know what was going on. And so, despite Ginsberg's characteristic deference —"It's Bill's book — whatever *he* says"[55] — in fact it's clear that *The Yage Letters* was, right to the end, determined as much by chance factors and the agency of others as by Burroughs himself.

Finally, the actual design of the book, including its cover, had evolved between late 1962 and early '63, and in this at least Burroughs did take an active lead. He was particularly inspired by the format of another project recently published by City Lights that Ginsberg had helped get going — Paul Bowles' collection of wonderful, kif-inspired Moroccan stories, *A Hundred Camels in the Courtyard*. The cover was simple but evocative, featuring Bowles' own black-and-white photographs of a kif pipe and a *naboula* arranged on a palm mat. "Liked the Bowles cover very much indeed," Burroughs told Ferlinghetti in September, adding, "I can send you a photomontage of my South American pictures."[56] The next month, Burroughs mailed him the image of a Makuna shaman, found in one of Schultes' *Harvard Botanical Museum* leaflets. Then in November he changed his mind again, and enclosed a photomontage set against a "background painting" by Brion Gysin.[57] Ferlinghetti was surely right to stick with the original image, however, and four decades later that shamanic figure remains on the cover of *The Yage Letters Redux* as an ever more haunting presence, the ghostly face of a rapidly vanishing world.

## "THE FINAL FIX"

*The Yage Letters Redux* reflects my conviction that the unexpectedly rich and complicated histories of the text's writing and publication needed to be told and put to practical use. Not that the record is now complete, any more than the re-edited text is now final and definitive. This is because the paradox true of all texts — that they are both fixed and flexible, defined in one form and context only to be redefined in another — is exactly what the historical record reveals so powerfully. *Redux* is a part of that historical process, not its perfect conclusion — not the "final fix."

If the text's histories of composition and publication turned out to be long and surprisingly complex, so too the challenges for editing. While the editor's basic task of presenting a reliable text can still be achieved—for example, by reexamining the manuscript of Ginsberg's 1960 letter to make the transcription more accurate—the goal of producing a unified and smoothly consistent text cannot. There's no single authoritative source to guide the editing of "In Search of Yage," given the state of Burroughs' original manuscript—"in rough form subject to corrections"—and the disappearance of its revised version. There have been times when finding a copy of that lost manuscript—stumbled upon, miscatalogued in some university archive, or pried from uncooperative private hands—has seemed like my own Grail quest. But if one day it should turn up, the life of the text will just be extended once again, and no doubt new mysteries will appear along with the new understandings.

Likewise, there are no simple solutions in the use of City Lights editions. While it appears straightforward to make the third edition the "base text" for the book's content—i.e., it offers the most complete version to work from—it is much more problematic to take it as the "copy text" for its "accidentals"— i.e., using its layout, punctuation and spelling as the default settings. As for the first edition, it alone has Burroughs' emphatic authorial approval (he wrote to Ferlinghetti, Ginsberg, and Ansen in early 1964 to praise it as "a model job of editing"),[58] as well as full records of corrected proofs and long galleys. But to recover that original is not an option: it would not only mean undoing the work of later editions and so denying the passage of time, but also erasing the larger textual history that came before the first edition and so decisively shaped it.[59]

Instead, I have gone back to basics, not to emend a particular previous text but to construct a new one, "word by word and punctuation mark by punctuation mark," as the textual scholar Thomas Tanselle puts it, "evaluating all the available evidence at each step."[60] And I have done so by complementing an authorial approach with a limited use of what theorists call "social text" editing. In principle, this means recognizing the authority of all textual collaborators — the various editors, from Creeley, Carroll, Hornick, Jones and Di Prima to Ferlinghetti, and other agents, like Alene Lee or John Sankey. Such recognition has important cultural implications — it highlights, for example, the neglected role of contributors other than white males (Lee, Jones, and Di Prima) — and this helps locate Burroughs and Ginsberg within an expanded field of collaborative activity. Equally, knowing the history of the text's composition and reception informs the process of editorial decision-making, although in practice the impact can be conservative as well as radical.

Let me clarify by giving some examples. Comparing *Redux* to the third edition, readers would quickly notice that I have, in effect, undone a very large number of punctuation changes that were intended to "correct" or "clarify" the meaning. It seemed to me that all these improvements (such as inserting thirty hyphens to make compound phrases) actually obscured a particular style, especially in "In Search of Yage," that allowed for ambiguity and imprecision and seemed to go with the fluid informality of epistolary form. The authority for preferring minimal punctuation couldn't rest with Burroughs' original rough manuscript, however — he expected it would be copy-edited by others — but depended on the historical record of the text published by City Lights and by *Black Mountain Review, Big Table, Kulchur* and *The Floating Bear* going back over thirty years.

These part-publications also have their own individual authority, however, so that in certain cases I have allowed contradictions to stand across the whole text in order to respect internal units of consistency. Take the layout of the letters on the page, which has always varied within and across City Lights editions quite arbitrarily. Setting them all out in a single standard format — as in the French edition, *Les lettres du Yage* (1967) — would create a misleading impression of overall coherence. Presenting each letter in the layout of their original magazine publications maintains the variety within the edition, while recognizing both the origins of the text in those publications and the internal consistency of each magazine's house-style.[61] Although they don't change the words that appear on the page, such matters are not inconsequential because they change the appearance of the page itself, a key part of any reader's experience of a book.

*Redux* makes a large number of changes and corrections—around 250 — most of which are small, although even a single misplaced digit or letter has material consequences — a drama acted out within "In Search of Yage," when Lee is arrested in Puerto Asís due to a mistake on his tourist card ("The consul in Panama had put down 52 instead of 53 in the date"). So for example, in all previous editions an extra zero created an oil pool in Texas "1000 miles across" — which made it larger than the state itself. Or take the spelling of place names such as "Mocoa" — previously always "Macoa" — or "Puerto Leguizamo" — previously "Leguisomo." These misspellings I have corrected, but not "Puerto Assis" because the most proper form — Puerto Asís — would require an accent (the same goes for Bogota, Puerto Limon, etc.), and it seemed to me that preserving the unpolished epistolary quality of the text should trump total accuracy. That's why the use of accents poses no problems in the "*Yagé* Article": the particular context and the specific history of the text suggest where to draw the line. Likewise, for the Appendices I have corrected

Burroughs' misspelling of *Banisteria caapi* (he always had double "n"), but not changed the term itself to *Banisteriopsis*, because it's revealing he didn't know that Spruce's classification had been corrected (by the taxonomist Morton, in 1931). To make the last correction would give the impression Burroughs knew something that at the time he didn't. Trying to recover history, editors have to be careful not to rewrite it.

As for the Appendix section, the idea for one actually goes back to 1962 when Ginsberg suggested that Ferlinghetti use selections from Alan Ansen's *Big Table* essay.[62] For my part, I have chosen to include previously unpublished primary materials, each with a particular status and relevance. Appendix 1 presents the only significant unused section of Burroughs' June 1953 "Yage" manuscript (while all unused individual lines or significant phrasings are given in the Endnotes), Appendix 2 presents the only unused material meant for insertion into that manuscript, and Appendix 3 presents possibly the only surviving section of Burroughs' December 1953 "Yage" manuscript. Appendices 4 and 5 present selections from Burroughs' 1956 "*Yagé* Article" (while other key lines are given in the Endnotes), important for reasons suggested earlier.

Finally, Appendix 6, selections transcribed from Ginsberg's journals around the time of his June 10, 1960 letter, appeared necessary for three reasons. Firstly, to contextualise the published letter and make possible comparisons between his journal and epistolary writing practice. Secondly, to clarify further his striking engagement with ayahuasca, such as his immediate grasp of how criminalizing its use was an attack on not only a people but a whole worldview. And lastly, although Ginsberg was right — in the end, it *is* Bill's book — and although that book is about many things other than *yagé*, nevertheless it seemed important as a way to recognize his crucial part in its composite authorship — as does letting Ginsberg have the last words here:

> A Materialistic consciousness is attempting to preserve itself from Dissolution by restriction & persecution of Experience of the Transcendental. One day perhaps the Earth will be dominated by the Illusion of Separate consciousness, the Bureaucrats having triumphed in seizing control of all roads of communication with the Divine, & restricting traffic. But Sleep & Death cannot evade the Great Dream of Being, and the victory of the Bureaucrats of Illusion is only an Illusion of their separate world of consciousness.

Oliver Harris
September 2005

[1] Professor Jim McLaverty, personal email, May 14, 2005.

[2] *Junkie* (New York: Ace, 1953) was published in unexpurgated form as *Junky* in 1977, and re-edited as *Junky: the definitive text of "Junk"* (New York: Penguin, 2003).

[3] Unless stated otherwise, all quotations of letters are from *The Letters of William S. Burroughs, 1945–1959* (New York: Viking, 1993).

[4] Campbell, *This is the Beat Generation* (London: Vintage, 2000), 144.

[5] In *Burroughs Live: The Collected Interviews of William S. Burroughs, 1960–1997*, edited by Sylvère Lotringer (Los Angeles: Semiotext(e), 2001), 29. Burroughs' own references are not much clearer or more credible: in *Queer*, Lee attributes his knowledge of the drug's telepathic powers vaguely to a couple of magazines; in his "*Yagé* Article," Burroughs is more precise, but his reference includes blatant fabrications, such as the comic name, "Colonel Frijoles Barbasco de Carne."

[6] Terrence McKenna, *Food of the Gods* (London: Random, 1992), 241.

[7] Schultes, "Botanical Sources of the New World Narcotics," *The Psychedelic Review* 1.2 (Fall 1963), 147.

[8] Ginsberg to Peter Orlovsky, August 3, 1961, in *Straight Hearts' Delight*, edited by Winston Leyland (San Francisco: Gay Sunshine, 1980), 207.

[9] Schultes, "An Overview of Hallucinogens in the Western Hemisphere," in *Flesh of the Gods*, edited by P.T. Furst (New York: Praeger, 1972), 3.

[10] Metzner, Introduction, *Ayahuasca: Hallucinogens, Consciousness, and the Spirit of Nature*, edited by Metzner (New York: Thunder's Mouth, 1999), 14.

[11] Schultes, *Vine of the Soul: Medicine Men, Their Plants and Rituals in the Colombian Amazonia* (New Mexico: Synergetic, 2004), 30.

[12] In *Burroughs Live*, 29, 25. Ginsberg got even less help from his lover, Peter Orlovsky, who wrote on the same day as Burroughs, only to say "I don't know what I can say" (in *Straight Hearts' Delight*, 199).

[13] Schultes, *Where the Gods Reign: Plants and Peoples of the Colombian Amazon* (London: Synergetic, 1988), 180.

[14] Schultes, "Recognition of Variability in Wild Plants by Indians of the Northwest Amazon: An Enigma," *Journal of Ethnobiology* 6.2 (Winter 1986), 238.

[15] Frederick Bois-Mariage, personal email, April 2005.

[16] Confusingly, in his "*Yagé* Article," Burroughs gives a different version, saying that the plant was "tentatively identified by a Peruvian botanist" (see Appendix 5).

[17] Manganotti, "The Final Fix," *Kulchur* 4.15 (Autumn 1964), 84–85.

[18] In *William S. Burroughs at the Front: Critical Reception, 1959–1989*, edited by Jennie Skerl and Robin Lydenberg (Carbondale: Southern Illinois UP, 1991), 35, 37.

[19] McKenna, *Food of the Gods*, 163.

[20] McKenna, *True Hallucinations: Being an Account of the Author's Extraordinary Adventures in the Devil's Paradise* (New York: HarperCollins, 1993), 70.

[21] Theroux, "Rumble in the Jungle," *The Guardian*, May 14, 2005.

[22] Ansen to Ginsberg, August 24, 1956 (Ginsberg Papers, Correspondence Series 1, Stanford University).

[23] In one of only three direct literary references in "In Search of Yage" (the others are to Truman Capote and Evelyn Waugh), Burroughs mentions H.G. Wells' "The Country of the Blind" (although he doesn't clarify that his 1904 tale is actually set in the Ecuadorian Cordilleras, in a lost valley not far from Bogotá). He seems to read it conventionally as a parable of individual creative vision imperiled    "But don't you understand? I can *see*"—when really it is a story about arrogant, short-sighted European imperialism.

[24] Burroughs, personal interview, November 1984.

[25] Murillo, *Colombia and the United States: War, Unrest and Destabilization* (New York: Seven Stories, 2004), 49.

[26] Guevara, *The Motorcycle Diaries: Notes on a Latin American Journey* (London: Harper Perennial, 2004), 157.

[27] Schultes, *Where the Gods Reign*, 21. When World War II broke out and the Japanese seized Malaysia, Schultes had volunteered his botanical expertise to find alternative sources of rubber, a strategically vital material. That research was what kept Schultes in the Amazon until Burroughs arrived a decade later.

[28] Morgan, *Literary Outlaw: The Life and Times of William S. Burroughs* (New York: Holt, 1988), 229.

[29] Burroughs to Ginsberg, January 19, 1953 (Ginsberg Collection, Columbia University—hereafter abbreviated as GC, CU).

[30] Burroughs to Ginsberg, April 30, 1953 (GC, CU).

[31] Burroughs to Ginsberg, May 4, 1953 (GC, CU).

[32] The picture is reproduced in Bill Morgan's *The Beat Generation in New York* (San Francisco: City Lights, 1997), 125.

[33] "I have no recollection of typing out *The Yage Letters* in 1953, nor do I remember Alene Lee." Personal letter, February 13, 2004.

[34] Ginsberg to Cowley, September 2, 1953 (GC, CU).

[35] Cowley to Ginsberg, September 10, 1953 (GC, CU).

[36] Ginsberg to Cowley, December 10, 1953 (GC, CU).

[37] *Letters to Allen Ginsberg, 1953–1957*, edited by Ron Padgett and Anne Waldman (New York: Full Court, 1982), 63.

[38] *Letters to Allen Ginsberg*, 80, 82.

[39] Ginsberg to Kerouac, February 17, 1955 (Miles Collection, Columbia University).

[40] "Tell Allen the piece of Burroughs I suggest," he wrote that September, "would be the whole vision of the Yage City." Kerouac, *Selected Letters, 1940–1956*, edited by Ann Charters (New York: Viking, 1995), 586.

[41] Ginsberg to Kerouac, October 9, 1957 (Miles Collection, Columbia University).

[42] Ginsberg to Ferlinghetti, September 3, 1957 (Correspondence Files, City Lights Records, 1955-1970, University of California, Berkeley — hereafter abbreviated as CLR, B).

[43] Ferlinghetti to Ginsberg, June 13, 1958 (GC, CU).

[44] Ginsberg to Ferlinghetti, June 26, 1962 (CLR, B).

[45] Bowles to Ferlinghetti, July 24, 1962 (CLR, B).

[46] Burroughs to Ferlinghetti, August 8, 1962 (CLR, B).

[47] Burroughs to Ferlinghetti, January 3, 1963 (CLR, B).

[48] Sankey to Ferlinghetti, October 8, 1963 (CLR, B).

[49] Burroughs to Ferlinghetti, November 22, 1975 (CLR, B).

[50] Ferlinghetti to Hardiment, June 1, 1963 (Burroughs-Hardiment Collection, Kansas University, Lawrence).

[51] Ferlinghetti to Ginsberg, June 11, 1963 (GC, CU).

[52] Actually, Ginsberg redrew (and elaborated) the images after Sankey pointed out that the original, on ruled paper, would not reproduce well.

[53] Ginsberg to Ferlinghetti, June 14, 1963 (CLR, B).

[54] Ferlinghetti to Ginsberg, June 28, 1963 (GC, CU).

[55] Ginsberg to Ferlinghetti, June 14, 1963 (CLR, B).

[56] Burroughs to Ferlinghetti, September 17, 1962 (CLR, B).

[57] Burroughs to Ferlinghetti, November 3, 1962 (CLR, B).

[58] Burroughs to Ferlinghetti, March 17, 1964 (CLR, B).

[59] I have also inspected every printing of *The Yage Letters* (twelve in all).

[60] Tanselle, "Textual Criticism at the Millenium," *Studies in Bibliography* 54, edited by David L. Vander Meulen (Charlottesville: UP of Virginia, 2003), 71.

[61] For more on the relation between the magazine part-publications and editing, see my article, "Not Burroughs' final fix: materializing *The Yage Letters*," in the e-journal, *Postmodern Culture* 16.3 (January 2006).

[62] Ginsberg to Ferlinghetti, September 19, 1962 (CLR, B).

# IN SEARCH OF YAGE (1953)

Dear Allen,

I stopped off here to have my piles out. Wouldn't do to go back among the Indians with piles I figured.

Bill Gains was in town and he has burned down the Republic of Panama from Las Palmas to David on paregoric. Before Gains, Panama was a P.G. town. You could buy four ounces in any drug store. Now the druggists are balky and the Chamber of Deputies was about to pass a special Gains Law when he threw in the towel and went back to Mexico. I was getting off junk and he kept nagging me why was I kidding myself once a junkie always a junkie. If I quit junk I would become a sloppy lush or go crazy taking cocaine.

One night I got lushed and bought some paregoric and he kept saying over and over, 'I *knew* you'd come home with paregoric. I *knew* it. You'll be a junkie all the rest of your life' and looking at me with his little cat smile. Junk is a cause with him.

I checked into the hospital junk sick and spent four days there. They would only give me three shots of morphine and I couldn't sleep from pain and heat and deprivation besides which there was a Panamanian hernia case in the same room with me and his friends came and stayed all day and half the night — one of them did in fact stay until midnight.

Recall walking by some American women in the corridor who looked like officers' wives. One of them was saying, 'I don't know why but I just can't eat sweets.'

'You got diabetes, lady,' I said. They all whirled around and gave me an outraged stare.

3

After checking out of the hospital, I stopped off at the U.S. Embassy. In front of the Embassy is a vacant lot with weeds and trees where boys undress to swim in the polluted waters of the bay—home of a small venomous sea snake. Smell of excrement and sea water and young male lust. No letters. I stopped again to buy two ounces of paregoric. Same old Panama. Whores and pimps and hustlers.

'Want nice girl?'

'Naked lady dance?'

'See me fuck my sister?'

No wonder food prices are high. They can't keep them down on the farm. They all want to come in the big city and be pimps.

I had a magazine article with me describing a joint outside Panama City called the Blue Goose. 'This is an anything goes joint. Dope peddlers lurk in the men's room with a hypo loaded and ready to go. Sometimes they dart out of a toilet and stick it in your arm without waiting for consent. Homosexuals run riot.'

The Blue Goose looks like a Prohibition era road house. A long one story building run down and covered with vines. I could hear frogs croaking from the woods and swamps around it. Outside a few parked cars, inside a dim bluish light. I remembered a Prohibition era road house of my adolescence and the taste of gin rickeys in a midwest Summer. (Oh my God! And the August moon in a violet sky and Billy Bradshinkel's cock. How sloppy can you get?)

Immediately two old whores sat down at my table without being asked and ordered drinks. The bill for one round was $6.90. The only thing lurking in the men's room was an insolent demanding lavatory attendant. I may add that far from running riot in Panama I never scored for one boy there. I wonder what a Panamanian boy would be like? Probably cut. When they say anything goes they are referring to the joint not the customers.

I ran into my old friend Jones the cab driver, and bought some C off him that was cut to hell and back. I nearly suffocated myself trying to sniff enough of this crap to get a lift. That's Panama. Wouldn't surprise me if they cut the whores with sponge rubber.

The Panamanians are about the crummiest people in the Hemisphere — I understand the Venezuelans offer competition — but I have never encountered any group of citizens that brings me down like the Canal Zone Civil Service. You cannot contact a civil servant on the level of intuition and empathy. He just does not have a receiving set, and he gives out like a dead battery. There must be a special low frequency civil service brain wave.

The Service men don't seem young. They have no enthusiasm and no conversation. In fact they shun the company of civilians. The only element in Panama I contact are the hip spades and they are all on the hustle.

Love,
Bill

P.S. Billy Bradshinkel got to be such a nuisance I finally had to kill him:

The first time was in my model A after the Spring prom. Billy with his pants down to his ankles and his tuxedo shirt still on, and jissom all over the car seat. Later I was holding his arm while he vomited in the car headlights, looking young and petulant with his blond hair mussed standing there in the warm spring wind. Then we got back in the car and turned the lights off and I said, 'Let's again.'

5

And he said, 'No we shouldn't.'

And I said, 'Why not?' and by then he was excited too so we did it again, and I ran my hands over his back under his tuxedo shirt and held him against me and felt the long baby hairs of his smooth cheek against mine and he went to sleep there and it was getting light when we drove home.

After that in the car several times and one time his family was away and we took off all our clothes and afterwards I watched him sleeping like a baby with his mouth a little open.

That Summer Billy caught typhoid and I went to see him every day and his mother gave me lemonade and once his father gave me a bottle of beer and a cigarette. When Billy was better we used to drive out to Creve Coeur Lake and rent a boat and go fishing and lie on the bottom of the boat with our arms around each other's shoulders not doing anything. One Saturday we explored an old quarry and found a cave and took our pants off in the musty darkness.

I remember the last time I saw Billy was in October of that year. One of those sparkling blue days you get in the Ozarks in Autumn. We had driven out into the country to hunt squirrels with my .22 single shot, and walked through the autumn woods without seeing anything to shoot at and Billy was silent and sullen and we sat on a log and Billy looked at his shoes and finally told me he couldn't see me again (notice I am sparing you the falling leaves).

'But why Billy? Why?'

'Well if you don't know I can't explain it to you. Let's go back to the car.'

We drove back in silence and when we came to his house he opened the door and got out. He looked at me for a second as if he was going to say something then turned abruptly and walked up the flagstone path to his house. I sat there for a minute looking at the closed door. Then I drove home feeling numb. When the car was stopped in the garage I put my head down on the wheel sobbing and rubbing my cheek against the steel spokes. Finally Mother called to me from an upstairs window was anything wrong and why didn't I come in the house. So I wiped the tears off my face and went in and said I was sick and went upstairs to bed. Mother brought me a bowl of milk toast on a tray but I couldn't eat any and cried all night.

After that I called Billy several times on the phone but he always hung up when he heard my voice. And I wrote him a long letter which he never answered.

Three months later when I read in the paper he had been killed in a car wreck and Mother said, 'Oh that's the Bradshinkel boy. You used to be such good friends didn't you?'

I said, 'Yes Mother' not feeling anything at all.

And I got a silo full of queer corn where that came from. Another routine: A man who manufactures memories to order. Any kind you want and he guarantees you'll believe they happened just that way—(As a matter of fact I have just about sold myself Billy Bradshinkel.) A line from the Japanese Sandman provides themesong of story, 'Just an old second hand man trading new dreams for old.' Ah what the hell! Give it to Truman Capote.

Another bit of reminiscence but genuine. Every Sunday at lunch my grandmother would disinter her dead brother killed 50 years ago when he dragged his shotgun through a fence and blew his lungs out.

7

'I always remember my brother such a lovely boy. I hate to see boys with guns.'

So every Sunday at lunch there was the boy lying by the wood fence and blood on the frozen red Georgia clay seeping into the winter stubble.

And poor old Mrs. Collins waiting for the cataracts to ripen so they can operate on her eye. Oh God! Sunday lunch in Cincinnati!

January 25, 1953
Hotel Nuevo Regis, Bogota

Dear Al,

Bogota is on a high plain surrounded by mountains. The grass of the savannah is bright green, and here and there black stone pre-Columbian monoliths are set up in the grass. A gloomy sombre looking town. My hotel room is a windowless cubicle (windows are a luxury in South America) with green composition board walls and the bed too short.

For a long time I sat there on the bed paralyzed with bum kicks. Then I walked out into the thin cold air to get a drink, thanking God I didn't hit this town junk sick. I had a few drinks and went back to the hotel where an ugly queer waiter served me an indifferent meal.

Next day I went to the University to get information on Yage. All sciences are lumped in The Institute. This is a red brick building, dusty corridors, unlabeled offices mostly locked. I climbed over crates and stuffed animals and botanical presses. These articles are continually being moved from one room to another for no discernible reason. People rush out of offices and claim some object from the litter in the hall and have it carried back into their offices. The porters sit around on crates smoking and greeting everybody as 'Doctor.'

In a vast dusty room full of plant specimens and the smell of formaldehyde, I saw a man looking for something he could not find with an air of refined annoyance. He caught my eye.

'Now what have they done with my cocoa specimens? It was a new species of wild cocoa. And what is this stuffed condor doing here on my table?'

The man had a thin refined face, steel rimmed glasses, tweed coat and dark flannel trousers. Boston and Harvard unmistakably. He introduced himself as Doctor Schindler. He was connected with a U.S. Agricultural Commission.

I asked about Yage. 'Oh yes,' he said, 'we have specimens here. Come along and I'll show you,' he said taking one last look for his cocoa. He showed me a dried specimen of the Yage vine which looked to be a very undistinguished sort of plant. Yes he had taken it. 'I got colors but no visions.'

He told me exactly what I would need for the trip, where to go and who to contact. I asked him about the telepathy angle. 'That's all imagination of course,' he said. He suggested the Putumayo as being the most readily accessible area where I could find Yage.

I took a few days to assemble my gear and dig the capitol. For a jungle trip you need medicines; snake bite serum, penicillin, entervioformo and aralen are essentials. A hammock, a blanket and a rubber bag known as a tula to carry your gear in.

Bogota is high and cold and wet, with a damp chill that gets inside you like the inner cold of junk sickness. There is no heat anywhere and you are never warm. In Bogota more than any other city I have seen in Latin America you feel the dead weight of Spain sombre and oppressive. Everything official bears the label Made in Spain.

As ever,
William

January 30
Hotel Niza, Pasto

Dear Al,

I took a bus to Cali because the autoferro was booked solid for days. Several times the cops shook down the bus and everybody on it. I had a gun in my luggage stashed under the medicines but they only searched my person at these stops. Obviously anyone carrying guns would bypass the stops or pack his guns where these sloppy laws wouldn't search. All they accomplish with the present system is to annoy the citizens. I never met anyone in Colombia who has a good word for the Policia Nacional.

The Policia Nacional is the Palace Guard of the Conservative Party (the army contains a good percentage of Liberals and is not fully trusted). This (the P.N.) is the most unanimously hideous body of young men I ever laid eyes on, my dear. They look like the end result of atomic radiation. There are thousands of these strange loutish young men in Colombia and I only saw one I would consider eligible and he looked ill at ease in his office.

If there is anything to say for the Conservatives I didn't hear it. They are an unpopular minority of ugly looking shits.

The road led over mountain passes down into the curious middle region of Tolima on the edge of the war zone. Trees and plains and rivers and more and more Policia Nacional. The population contains some of the best looking and the ugliest people I ever saw. Most of them seemed to have nothing better to do than stare at the bus and the passengers and especially at the gringo. They would stare at me until I smiled or waved, then smile back the predatory toothless smile that greets the American all through South America.

'Hello Mister. One cigarette?'

In a hot dusty coffee stop town I saw a boy with delicate copper features, beautiful soft mouth and teeth far apart in bright red gums. Fine black hair fell in front of his face. His whole person exuded a sweet masculine innocence.

At one customs stop I met a nacional law who had fought in Korea. He pulled open his shirt to show me the scars on his unappetizing person.

'I like you guys,' he said.

I never feel flattered by this promiscuous liking for Americans. It is insulting to individual dignity, and no good ever comes from these America lovers.

In the late afternoon I bought a bottle of brandy and got drunk with the bus driver. Stopped over in Armenia and went on to Cali next day with the autoferro.

Vegetation semitropical with bamboo and bananas and papayas, Cali is a relatively pleasant town with a nice climate. You do not feel tension here. Cali has a high rate of straight non political crime. Even safe crackers. (Big operators in the crime are rare in South America.)

I met some old time American residents who said the country was in a hell of a shape.

'They hate the sight of a foreigner down here. You know why? It's all this Point Four and good nabor crap and financial aid. If you give these people anything they think "oh so he needs me." And the more you give the bastards the nastier they get.'

I heard this line from old timers all over S.A. It does not occur to them that something more basic is involved here than the activities of Point Four. Like the U.S. Pegler fans say, 'The trouble is Unions.' They would still say it spitting blood from radiation sickness. Or in process of turning into crustaceans.

On to Popayan by autoferro. This is a quiet university town. Someone told me the place was full of intellectuals but I did not see any. A curious, negativistic hostility pervades the place. Walking in the main square a man bumped into me with no apology, his face blank, catatonic.

I was drinking coffee in a cafe where a young man with an archaic Jewish-Assyrian face approached me and went into a long spiel about how much he liked foreigners and how he wanted to buy me a drink or at least pay for my coffee. As he talked it became obvious that he did not like foreigners and had no intention of buying me a drink. I paid for my coffee and left.

In another cafe some gambling game like bingo was in progress. A man came in emitting curious yelps of imbecile hostility. Nobody looked up from their bingo.

In front of the post office were Conservative posters. One of them read: 'Farmers, the army is fighting for your welfare. Crime degrades a man and he can't live with himself. Work elevates him towards God. Cooperate with the police and the military. *They only need your information.*' (Italics mine.)

It's your duty to turn in the guerrillas and work and know your place and listen to the priest. What an old con! Like trying to sell the Brooklyn Bridge. Not many people are buying it. The majority of Colombians are Liberals.

The Policia Nacional slouch on every corner, awkward and self-conscious, waiting to shoot somebody or do anything but stand there under hostile eyes. They have a huge gray wagon that rides around and around the town with no prisoners in it.

I walked out along a dusty road. Rolling country with green grass, cattle and sheep and small farms. A horribly diseased cow was standing in the road covered with dust. A roadside shrine with a glass front. The ghastly pinks and blues and yellows of religious art.

Saw a movie short about a priest in Bogota, runs a brick factory and makes homes for the workers. The short shows the priest fondling the bricks and patting the workers on the back and generally putting down the old Catholic con. A thin man with distraught neurotic eyes. Finally he gave a speech to the effect: Wherever you find social progress or good works or anything good there you will find the Church.

His speech had nothing to do with what he was really saying. There was no mistaking the neurotic hostility in his eyes, the fear and hate of life. He sat there in his black uniform nakedly revealed as the advocate of death. A business man without the motivation of avarice, cancerous activity sterile and blighting. Fanaticism without fire or energy exuding a musty odor of spiritual decay. He looked sick and dirty — though I guess he was clean enough actually — with a suggestion of yellow teeth, unwashed underwear and psychosomatic liver trouble. I wonder what his sex life could be.

Another short showed a get together of the Conservative party. They all looked congealed, a frozen crust on the country. The audience sat there in complete silence. Not a murmur of approval or dissent. Nothing. Naked propaganda falling flat in dead silence.

Next day took a bus for Pasto. Driving in, the place hit me in the stomach with a physical impact of depression and horror. High mountains all around. High thin air. The inhabitants peering out of sod roofed huts, their eyes red with smoke. The hotel was Swiss run and excellent. I walked around the town. Ugly crummy looking populace. The higher you get the uglier the citizens. This is a leprosy area. (Leprosy in Colombia is more prevalent in high mountains, T.B. on the coast.) It seemed like every second person had a harelip or one leg shorter than the other or a blind festering eye.

I went into a cantina and drank aguardiente and played the mountain music on the juke box. There is something archaic in this music strangely familiar, very old and very sad. Decidedly not Spanish in origin, nor is it oriental. Shepherd music played on a bamboo instrument like a panpipe, pre-classic, Etruscan perhaps. I have heard similar music in the mountains of Albania where pre-Greek, Illyrian racial strains linger. A phylogenetic nostalgia conveyed by this music — Atlantean?

I saw working behind the bar what looked at first like an attractive boy of 14 or so (the place was dimly lit owing to a partial power failure). Going over by the bar for a closer look, I saw his face was old, his body swollen with pith and water like a rotten melon.

An Indian was sitting at the next table fumbling in his pockets, his fingers numb with alcohol. It took him several minutes to pull out some crumpled bills — what my grandmother, a violent prohibitionist, used to describe as 'dirty money' — he caught my eye and smiled a twisted broken smile. 'What else can I do?'

In one corner a young Indian was pawing a whore, an ugly woman with a bestial ill-natured face and the dirty light pink dress of her calling. Finally she disengaged herself and walked out. The young Indian looked after her in silence without anger. She was gone and that was that. He walked over to the drunk and helped him up and together they staggered out with the sad sweet resignation of the mountain Indian.

I had an introduction from Schindler to a German who runs a wine factory in Pasto. I found him in a room full of books warmed by two electric heaters. The first heat I had seen in Colombia. He had a thin ravaged face, sharp nose, downcurving mouth, a junkie mouth. He was very sick. Heart bad, kidneys bad, high blood pressure.

'And I used to be tough as nails,' he said plaintively. 'What I want to do is go to the Mayo Clinic. A doctor here gave me an injection of iodine which upset my whole metabolism. If I eat anything with salt my feet swell up like that.'

Yes he knew the Putumayo well. I asked about Yage.

'Yes, I sent some to Berlin. They made tests and reported the effect is identical to the effect of hashish . . . there is a bug in the Putumayo, I forget what they call it, like a big grasshopper, such a powerful aphrodisiac, if it flies on you and you can't get a woman right away you will die. I have seen them running around jacking off from contact with this animal . . . I have one in alcohol around some place . . . no, come to think it was lost when I moved here after the war . . . another thing I have been trying to get information on it . . . a vine you chew and all your teeth fall out.'

'Just the thing for practical jokes on your friends,' I said.

The maid brought in tea and pumpernickel and sweet butter on a tray.

'I hate this place but what is a fellow to do? I have my business here. My wife. I'm stuck.'

Will leave here in next few days for Mocoa and the Putumayo. Won't write from there since mail service beyond Pasto is extremely unreliable depending on volunteer carrier-bus and truck drivers mostly. More letters are lost than delivered. These people do not have even the concept of responsibility.

As Ever,
Willy Lee

February 28, 1953
Hotel Niza, Pasto

Dear Allen:

On my way back to Bogota with nothing accomplished. I have been conned by medicine men (the most inveterate drunk, liar and loafer in the village is invariably the medicine man), incarcerated by the law, rolled by a local hustler (I thought I was getting that innocent backwoods ass, but the kid had been to bed with six American oil men, a Swedish Botanist, a Dutch Ethnographer, a Capuchin father known locally as The Mother Superior, a Bolivian Trotskyite on the lam, and jointly fucked by the Cocoa Commission and Point Four). Finally I was prostrated by malaria. I will relate events more or less chronologically.

I took a bus to Mocoa which is the capital of the Putumayo and end of the road. From there on you go by mule or canoe. For some reason these end of road towns are always God awful. Anyone expecting to outfit himself there will find they have nothing he needs in the stores. Not even citronella — and no one in these end of the road towns knows anything about the jungle.

I arrived in Mocoa late at night and consumed a ghastly Colombian soft drink under the dubious eyes of a nacional cop who could not make up his mind whether to question me or not. Finally he got up and left and I went to bed. The night was cool, about like Puyo, another awful end of the road town.

When I woke up next morning I began to get bum kicks still in bed. I looked out the window. Cobble stone, muddy streets, one story buildings mostly shops. Nothing out of the ordinary but in all my experience as a traveler — and I have seen some God awful places — no place ever brought me down like Mocoa. And I don't know exactly why.

Mocoa has about 2000 inhabitants and sixty nacional cops. One of them rides around all day through the four streets of the town on a motor bicycle. You can hear him from any place in town. Radios with extra loud speakers in every cantina make a horrible discordant noise (there are no juke boxes in Mocoa where you can play what you want to hear). The police have a brass band they bang around three or four times a day starting in the early morning. I never saw any signs of disorder in this town which is well out of the war zone. But there is an air of unresolved and insoluble tension about Mocoa, the agencies of control out in force to put down an uprising which does not occur. Mocoa is The End Of The Road. A final stalemate with the cop riding around and around on his motor bicycle for all eternity.

17

I went on to Puerto Limon which is about 30 miles from Mocoa. This town can be reached by truck. Here I located an intelligent Indian and ten minutes later I had a Yage vine. But the Indian would not prepare it since this is a monopoly of the Brujo (medicine man).

This old drunken fraud was crooning over a man evidently down with malaria. (Maybe he was chasing the evil spirit out of his patient and into the gringo. Anyway I came down with malaria two weeks to the day later.) The Brujo told me he had to be half lushed up to work his witchcraft and cure people. The high cost of liquor was working a hardship on the sick, he was only hitting two cylinders on a short count of lush. I bought him a pint of aguardiente and he agreed to prepare the Yage for another quart. He did in fact prepare a pint of cold water infusion after misappropriating half the vine so that I did not notice any effect.

That night I had a vivid dream in color of the green jungle and a red sunset I had seen during the afternoon. Also a composite city familiar to me but I could not quite place it. Part New York, part Mexico City and part Lima which I had not seen at this time. I was standing on a corner by a wide street with cars going by and a vast open park down the street in the distance. I cannot say whether these dreams had any connection with Yage. Incidentally you are supposed to see a city when you take Yage.

I spent a day in the jungle with an Indian guide to dig the jungle and collect some Yoka, a vine the Indians use to prevent hunger and fatigue during long trips in the jungle. In fact, some of them use it because they are too lazy to eat.

The Upper Amazon jungle has fewer disagreeable features than the midwest Stateside woods in Summer. Sand flies and jungle mosquitoes are

18

the only outstanding pests and you can keep them off with insect repellent. I didn't have any at this time. I never got any ticks or chiggers in the Putumayo. The trees are tremendous, some of them 200 feet tall. Walking under these trees I felt a special silence, a vibrating soundless hum. We waded through clear streams of water (who started this story you can't drink jungle water? Why not?).

Yoka grows on high ground and it took us four hours to get there. The Indian cut a Yoka vine and shaved off a handful of the inner bark with a machete. He soaked the bark in a little cold water, squeezed the water out of the bark and handed me the infusion in a palm leaf cup. It was faintly bitter but not unpleasant. In ten minutes I felt a tingling in my hands and a nice lift somewhat like benzedrine but not so tight. I walked the four hours back over jungle trail without stopping and could have walked twice that far.

After a week in Puerto Limon I went to Puerto Umbria by truck and down to Puerto Assis by canoe. These canoes are about 30 feet long with an outboard motor. This is standard method of travel on the Putumayo. The motors are out of commission about half the time. This is because people take them apart and leave out the pieces they consider non-essential. Also they economize on grease so the motors burn out.

I arrived in Puerto Assis at 10 p.m. and as soon as I stepped out of the canoe a federal cop wanted to see my papers. There is more check on papers in the quiet zones like Putumayo than in Villavicencio which is edge of the war zone. In the Putumayo you won't be five minutes in any whistle stop before they check your papers. They expect trouble to come from outside in the form of a foreigner — God knows why.

Next day the governor, who looked like a degenerate strain of monkey, found an error in my tourist card. The consul in Panama had put down 52 instead of 53 in the date. I tried to explain this was an error, clear enough in view of the dates on my plane tickets, passport, receipts, but the man was bone stupid. I don't think he understands yet. So the cop gave my luggage a shake missing the gun but decided to impound the medicine gun and all. The sanitary inspector put in his two cents suggesting they go through the medicines.

'For God's sake,' I thought. 'Go inspect an outhouse.'

They informed me I was under town arrest pending a decision from Mocoa. So I was stuck in Puerto Assis with nothing to do but sit around all day and get drunk every night. I had planned to take a canoe trip up the Rio Guaymes to contact the Kofan Indians who are known Yage artists, but the governor would not let me leave Puerto Assis.

Puerto Assis is a typical Putumayo River town. A mud street along the river, a few shops, one cantina, a mission where Capuchin fathers lead the life of Riley, a hotel called the Putumayo where I was housed.

The hotel was run by a whorish looking landlady. Her husband was a man of about 40, powerful and vigorous but there was a beat look in his eyes. They had seven daughters and you could tell by looking at him that he would never have a son. At least not by that woman. This giggling brood of daughters kept coming into my room (there was no door, only a thin curtain) to watch me dress and shave and brush my teeth. It was a bum kick. And I was the victim of idiotic pilfering—a catheter tube from my medical kit, a jock strap, vitamin B tablets.

There was a boy in town who had once acted as a guide to an American naturalist. This boy was the local Mister Specialist. You find one of these pests all over South America. They can say, 'Hello Joe' or

'O.K.' or 'Fucky fucky.' Many of them refuse to speak Spanish thus limiting conversation to sign language.

I was sitting on a worn out inverted canoe that serves as a bench in the main drag of Puerto Assis. The boy came and sat with me and began talking about the Mister who collected animals, 'He collected spiders, and scorpions and snakes.' I was half asleep lulled by this litany when I heard, 'And he was going to take me back to the States with him,' and woke up. 'Oh God,' I thought, 'that old line.'

The boy smiled at me showing gaps in his front teeth. He moved a little closer on the bench. I could feel my stomach tighten.

'I have a good canoe,' he said. 'Why don't you let me take you up the Guaymes? I know all the Indians up there.'

He looked like the most inefficient guide in the Upper Amazon but I said, 'Yes.'

That night I saw the boy in front of the cantina. He put his arms around my shoulders and said, 'Come in and have a drink, Mister,' letting his hand slip down my back and off my ass.

We went in and got drunk under the weary wise eyes of the bartender and took a walk out along the jungle trail. We sat down in the moonlight by the side of the trail and he let his elbow fall into my crotch and said, 'Mister,' next thing I heard was, 'How much you gonna give me?'

He wanted $30 evidently figuring he was a rare commodity in the Upper Amazon. I beat him down to $10 bargaining under increasingly disadvantageous conditions. Somehow he managed to roll me for $20 and my underwear shorts (when he told me to take my underwear all the way off I thought, a passionate type, my dear, but it was only a maneuver to steal my skivvies).

After five days in Puerto Assis I was well on the way to establish myself as a citizen in the capacity of village wastrel. Meanwhile sepulchral telegrams issued periodically from Mocoa. 'The case of the foreigner from Ohio will be resolved.' And finally, 'Let the foreigner from Ohio be returned to Mocoa.'

So I went back up the river with the cop (I was technically under arrest). In Puerto Umbria I came down with chills and fever. Arriving in Mocoa on a Sunday, the Commandante was not there so the second in command had me locked up in a wood cubicle without even a bucket to piss in. They put all my gear unsearched in with me. A typical South American touch. I could have had a machine gun concealed in my luggage. I took some aralen and lay down shivering under the blanket. The man in the next cell was confined for lack of some document. I never did understand the details of his case. Next morning the Commandante showed up and I was summoned to his office. He shook hands pleasantly, looked at my papers, and listened to my explanation.

'Clearly an error,' he said. 'This man is free.' What a pleasure it is to encounter an intelligent man in such circumstances.

I went back to the hotel and went to bed and called a doctor. He took my temperature and said, 'Caramba!' and gave me an injection of quinine and liver extract to offset secondary anemia. I continued the aralen. I had some codeine tablets to control malaria headache so I lay there sleeping most of the time for three days.

I will go to Bogota, have my tourist card reassembled and return here. Travel in Colombia is difficult even with the soundest credentials. I have never seen such ubiquitous and annoying police. You are supposed to register with the police wherever you go. This is unpardonable stupidity. If I was an active Liberal what could I do in Puerto Assis aside from taking the place over at gun point?

As Ever,
William


March 3
Hotel Nuevo Regis, Bogota

Dear Al:

Bogota horrible as ever. I had my papers corrected with the aid of U.S. Embassy. Figure to sue the truss off PAA for fucking up the tourist card.

I have attached myself to an expedition — in a somewhat vague capacity to be sure — consisting of Doc Schindler, two Colombian Botanists, two English Broom Rot specialists from the Cocoa Commission, and will return to the Putumayo in convoy. Will write full account of trip when I get back to this town for the third time.

As Ever,
Bill

April 15

Hotel Nuevo Regis, Bogota

Dear Al:

Back in Bogota. I have a crate of Yage. I have taken it and know more or less how it is prepared. By the way you may see my picture in *Exposure*. I met a reporter going in as I was going out. Queer to be sure but about as appetizing as a hamper of dirty laundry. Not even after two months in the brush, my dear. This character is shaking down the South American continent for free food and transport, and discounts on everything he buys with a 'We-got-like-two-kinds-of-publicity-favorable-and-unfavor-able-which-do-you-want,-Jack?' routine. What a shameless mooch. But who am I to talk?

Flashback: Retraced my journey through Cali, Popayan and Pasto to Mocoa. I was interested to note that Mocoa dragged Schindler and the two Englishmen as much as it did me.

This trip I was treated like visiting royalty under the misapprehension I was a representative of the Texas Oil Company travelling incognito. (Free boat rides, free plane rides, free chow; eating in the officers' mess, sleeping in the governor's house.)

The Texas Oil Company surveyed the area a few years ago, found no oil and pulled out. But everyone in the Putumayo believes the Texas Company will return. Like the second coming of Christ. The governor told me the Texas Company had taken two samples of oil 80 miles apart and it was the same oil, so there was a pool of the stuff 80 miles across under Mocoa. I heard this same story in a back water area of East Texas where the oil company made a survey and found no oil and pulled out. Only in Texas the pool was 100 miles across. The beat town psyche is

24

joined the world over like the oil pool. You take a sample anywhere and it's the same shit. And the governor thinks they are about to build a rail-road from Pasto to Mocoa, and an airport. As a matter of fact the whole Putumayo region is on the down grade. The rubber business is shot, the cocoa is eaten up with broom rot, no price on rotenone since the war, land is poor and there is no way to get produce out. The dawdling psychophrenia of small town boosters. Like I should think some day soon boys will start climbing in through the transom and tunneling under the door.

Several times when I was drunk I told someone, 'Look. There is no oil here. That's why Texas pulled out. They won't ever come back. Understand?' But they couldn't believe it.

We went out to visit a German who owned a finca near Mocoa. The British went looking for wild coca with an Indian guide. I asked the German about Yage.

'Sure,' he said. 'My Indians all use it.' A half hour later I had 20 pounds of Yage vine. No trek through virgin jungle and some old white haired character saying, 'I have been expecting you my son.' A nice German 10 minutes from Mocoa.

The German also made a date for me to take Yage with the local Brujo (at that time I had no idea how to prepare it).

The medicine man was around 70 with a baby smooth face. There was a sly gentleness about him like an old-time junkie. It was getting dark when I arrived at his dirt floor thatch shack for my Yage appointment. First thing he asked did I have a bottle? I brought a quart of aguardiente out of my knapsack and handed it to him. He took a long drink and passed the bottle to his assistant. I didn't take any as I wanted straight Yage kicks. The Brujo put the bottle beside him and squatted down by a bowl set on a tripod. Behind the bowl was a wood shrine with a picture of the Virgin, a crucifix, a wood idol, feathers and little packages tied with ribbons. The Brujo sat there a long time without moving. He took another long swig on the bottle. The women retired behind a bamboo partition and were not seen again. The Brujo began crooning over the bowl. I caught 'Yage Pintar' repeated over and over. He shook a little broom over the bowl and made a swishing noise. This is to whisk away evil spirits who might slip in the Yage. He took a drink and wiped his mouth and went on crooning. You can't hurry a Brujo. Finally he uncovered the bowl and dipped about an ounce more or less of black liquid which he handed me in a dirty red plastic cup. The liquid was oily and phosphorescent. I drank it straight down. Bitter foretaste of nausea. I handed the cup back and the medicine man and the assistant took a drink.

I sat there waiting for results and almost immediately had the impulse to say, 'That wasn't enough. I need more.' I have noticed this inexplicable impulse on the two occasions when I got an overdose of junk. Both times before the shot took effect I said, 'That wasn't enough. I need more.'

Roy told me about a man who came out of jail clean and nearly died in Roy's room. 'He took the shot and right away said, "That wasn't enough" and fell on his face out cold. I dragged him out in the hall and called an ambulance. He lived.'

In two minutes a wave of dizziness swept over me and the hut began spinning. It was like going under ether, or when you are very drunk and lie down and the bed spins. Blue flashes passed in front of my eyes. The hut took on an archaic far-Pacific look with Easter Island heads carved in the support posts. The assistant was outside lurking there with the obvious intent to kill me. I was hit by violent, sudden nausea and rushed for the door hitting my shoulder against the door post. I felt the shock but no pain. I could hardly walk. No coordination. My feet were like blocks of wood. I vomited violently leaning against a tree and fell down on the ground in helpless misery. I felt numb as if I was covered with layers of cotton. I kept trying to break out of this numb dizziness. I was saying over and over, 'All I want is out of here.' An uncontrollable mechanical silliness took possession of me. Hebephrenic meaningless repetitions. Larval beings passed before my eyes in a blue haze, each one giving an obscene, mocking squawk (I later identified this squawking as the croaking of frogs) — I must have vomited six times. I was on all fours convulsed with spasms of nausea. I could hear retching and groaning as if it was someone else. I was lying by a rock. Hours must have passed. The medicine man was standing over me. I looked at him for a long time before I believed he was really there saying, 'Do you want to come into the house?' I said, 'No,' and he shrugged and went back inside.

My arms and legs began to twitch uncontrollably. I reached for my nembutals with numb wooden fingers. It must have taken me ten minutes to open the bottle and pour out five capsules. Mouth was dry but I chewed the nembutals down somehow. The twitching spasms subsided slowly and I felt a little better and went into the hut. The blue flashes still in front of my eyes. Lay down and covered myself with a blanket. I had a chill like malaria. Suddenly very drowsy. Next morning I was all right except for a feeling of lassitude and a slight backlog of nausea. I paid off the Brujo and walked back to town.

We all went down to Puerto Assis that day. Schindler kept complaining the Putumayo had deteriorated since he was there ten years ago. 'I never made a Botanical expedition like this before,' he said. 'All these farms and *people*. You have to walk miles to get to the jungle.'

Schindler had two assistants to carry his luggage, cut down trees and press specimens. One of them was an Indian from the Vaupes region where the method of preparing Yage is different from the Putumayo Kofan method. In Putumayo the Indians cut the vines into eight inch pieces using about five sections to a person. The pieces of vine are crushed with a rock and boiled with a double handful of leaves from another plant — tentatively identified as ololuiqui — the mixture is boiled all day with a small amount of water and reduced to about two ounces of liquid.

In the Vaupes the bark is scraped off about three feet of vine to form a large double handful of shavings. The bark is soaked in a liter of cold water for several hours, and the liquid strained off and taken over a period of an hour. No other plant is added.

I decided to try some Yage prepared Vaupes method. The Indian and I started scraping off bark with machetes (the inner bark is the most active). This is white and sappy at first but almost immediately turns red on expo- sure to air. The landlady's daughters watched us pointing and giggling. This is strictly against Putumayo Protocol for the preparation of Yage. The Brujo of Mocoa told me if a woman witnesses the preparation the Yage spoils on the spot and will poison anyone who drinks it or at least drive him insane. The old women-are-dirty-and-under-certain-circumstances- poisonous routine. I figured this was a chance to test the woman pollution myth once and for all with seven female creatures breathing down my neck, poking sticks in the mixture, fingering the Yage and giggling.

The cold water infusion is a light red color. That night I drank a quart of infusion over a period of one hour. Except for blue flashes and slight nausea—though not to the point of vomiting—the effect was similar to weed. Vividness of mental imagery, aphrodisiac results, silliness and giggling. In this dosage there was no fear, no hallucinations or loss of control. I figure this dose as about one third the dose that the Brujo gave me.

Next day we went on down to Puerto Espina where the governor put us up in his house. That is we slung our hammocks in empty rooms on the top floor. A coolness arose between the Colombians and the British because the Colombians refused to get up for an early start, and the British complained the Cocoa Commission was being sabotaged by a couple of 'lazy spics.'

Every day we plan to get an early start for the jungle. About 11 o'clock the Colombians finish breakfast (the rest of us waiting around since 8) and begin looking for an incompetent guide, preferably someone with a finca near town. About 1 we arrive at the finca and spend another hour eating lunch. Then the Colombians say, 'They tell us the jungle is far. About three hours. We don't have time to make it today.' So we start back to town, the Colombians collecting a mess of plants along the way. 'So long as they can collect any old weed they don't give a ruddy fuck,' one of the Englishmen said to me after an expedition to the nearest finca.

There was supposed to be plane service out of Puerto Espina. Schindler and I were ready to go back to Bogota at this point, so there we sit in Puerto Espina waiting on this plane and the agent doesn't have a radio or any way of finding out when the plane gets there if it gets there and he says, 'Sure as shit boys one of these days you'll look up and see the Catalina coming in over the river flashing in the sun like a silver fish.'

So I says to Doc Schindler, 'We could grow old and simple-minded sitting around playing dominoes before any sonofabitching plane sets down here and the river getting higher every day and how to get back up it with every motor in Puerto Espina broke?'

(The citizens who own these motor canoes spend all the time fiddling with their motors and taking the motors apart and leaving out pieces they consider non-essential so the motors never run. The boat owners do have a certain Rube Goldberg ingenuity in patching up the stricken motor for one last more spurt—but this was a question of going up the river. Going down river you will get there eventually motor or no, but coming up river you gotta have some means of propulsion.)

Sure you think it's romantic at first but wait 'til you sit there five days onna sore ass sleeping in Indian shacks and eating Yoka and some hunka nameless meat like the smoked pancreas of a two toed sloth and all night you hear them fiddle fucking with the motor—they got it bolted to the porch — 'buuuuurt spluuuu . . . . ut . . . . spluuuu . . . . ut,' and you can't sleep hearing the motor start and die all night and then it starts to rain. Tomorrow the river will be higher.

So I says to Schindler, 'Doc, I'll float down to the Atlantic before I start back up that fucking river.'

And he says, 'Bill, I haven't been fifteen years in this sonofabitch country and lost all my teeth in the service without picking up a few angles. Now down yonder in Puerto Leguizamo — they got like military planes and I happen to know the Commandante is Latah.' (Latah is a condition occurring in South East Asia. Otherwise normal, the Latah cannot help doing whatever anyone tells him to do once his attention has been attracted by touching him or calling his name.)

So Schindler went on down to Puerto Leguizamo while I stayed in Puerto Espina waiting to hitch a ride with the Cocoa Commission. Every

30

day I saw that plane agent and he came on with the same bullshit. He showed me a horrible looking scar on the back of his neck. 'Machete,' he said. No doubt some exasperated citizen who went berserk waiting on one of his planes.

The Colombians and the Cocoa Commission went up the San Miguel and I was alone in Puerto Espina eating in the Commandante's house. God awful greasy food. Rice and fried platano cakes three times a day. I began slipping the platanos in my pocket and throwing them away later. The Commandante kept telling me how much Schindler liked this food — (Schindler is an old South American hand. He can really put down the bullshit) — did I like it? I would say, 'Magnificent,' my voice cracking. Not enough I have to eat his greasy food. I have to say I like it.

The Commandante knew from Schindler I had written a book on 'marijuana.' From time to time I saw suspicion seep into his dull liverish eyes.

'Marijuana degenerates the nervous system,' he said looking up from a plate of platanos.

I told him he should take Vitamin B1 and he looked at me as if I had advocated the use of a narcotic.

The governor regarded me with cold disfavor because one of the gasoline drums belonging to the Cocoa Commission had leaked on his porch. I was expecting momentarily to be evicted from the governmental mansion.

The Cocoa Commission and the Colombians came back from the San Miguel in a condition of final estrangement. It seems the Colombians had found a finca and spent three days there lolling about in their pajamas. In the absence of Schindler I was the only buffer between the two factions and suspect by both parties of secretly belonging to the other (I had bor-

31

rowed a shotgun from one of the Colombians and was riding in the Cocoa Commission boat).

We went on down the river to Puerto Leguizamo where the Commandante put us up in a gun boat anchored in the Putumayo. There were no guns on it actually. I think it was the hospital ship.

The ship was dirty and rusty. The water system did not function and the W.C. was in unspeakable condition. The Colombians run a mighty loose ship. It wouldn't surprise me to see someone shit on the deck and wipe his ass with the flag. (This derives from a dream that came to me in 17th century English. 'The English and French delegates did shit on the floor, and tearing the Treaty of Seville into strips with much merriment did wipe their backsides with it, seeing which the Spanish delegate withdrew from the conference.')

Puerto Leguizamo is named for a soldier who distinguished himself in the Peruvian War of 1940. I asked one of the Colombians about it and he nodded, 'Yes, Leguizamo was a soldier who did something in the war.'

'What did he do?'

'Well, he did *something.*'

The place looks like it was left over from a receding flood. Rusty abandoned machinery scattered here and there. Swamps in the middle of town. Unlighted streets you sink up to your knees in.

There are five whores in town sitting out in front of blue walled cantinas. The young kids of Puerto Leguizamo cluster around the whores with the immobile concentration of tom cats. The whores sit there in the muggy night under one naked electric bulb in the blare of juke box music, waiting.

Inquiring in the environs of Puerto Leguizamo I found the use of

Yage common among both Indians and whites. Most everybody grows it in his backyard.

After a week in Leguizamo I got a plane to Villavicencio, and from there back to Bogota by bus.

So here I am back in Bogota. No money waiting for me (check apparently stolen), I am reduced to the shoddy expedient of stealing my drinking alcohol from the university laboratory placed at disposal of the visiting scientist.

Extracting Yage alkaloids from the vine, a relatively simple process according to directions provided by the Institute. My experiments with extracted Yage have not been conclusive. I do not get blue flashes or any pronounced sharpening of mental imagery. Have noticed aphrodisiac effects. The extract makes me sleepy whereas the fresh vine is a stimulant and in overdose convulsive poison.

Every night I go into a cafe and order a bottle of Pepsi-Cola and pour in my lab alcohol. The population of Bogota lives in cafes. There are any number of these and always full. Standard dress for Bogota cafe society is a gabardine trench coat and of course suit and tie. A South American's ass may be sticking out of his pants but he will still have a tie.

Bogota is essentially a small town, everybody worrying about his clothes and looking as if he would describe his job as responsible. I was sitting in one of these white collar cafes when a boy in a filthy light gray suit, but still clinging to a frayed tie, asked me if I spoke English.

I said, 'Fluently,' and he sat down at the table. A former employee of the Texas Company. Obviously queer, blond, German looking, European manner. We went to several cafes. He pointed people out to me saying, 'He doesn't want to know me any more now that I am without work.'

These people, correctly dressed and careful in manner, did in fact look away and in some cases call for the bill and leave. I don't know how the boy could have looked any less queer in a $200 suit.

One night I was sitting in a Liberal cafe when three civilian Conservative gun men came in yelling 'Viva los Conservadores' hoping to provoke somebody so they could shoot him. There was a middle aged man of the type who features a loud mouth. The others sat back and let him do the yelling. The other two were youngish, ward heelers, corner boys, borderline hoodlums. Narrow shoulders, ferret faces and smooth, tight, red skin, bad teeth. It was almost too pat. The two hoodlums looked a little hang dog and ashamed of themselves like the young man in the limerick who said, 'I'll admit I'm a bit of a shit.'

Everybody paid and walked out leaving the loud mouthed character yelling 'Viva El Partido Conservador' to an empty house.

As Ever,
Bill


May 5
930 Jose Leal, Lima

Dear Allen:

This finds me in Lima which is enough like Mexico City to make me homesick. Mexico is home to me and I can't go there. Got a letter from my lawyer—I am sentenced in absentia. I feel like a Roman exiled from Rome. Plan to hit Peru jungle for additional Yage material. Will spend a few weeks digging Lima.

Went through Ecuador fast as possible. What an awful place it is. Small country national inferiority complex in most advanced stage.

Ecuadorian Miscellanea: *Esmeraldas* hot and wet as a Turkish bath and vultures eating a dead pig in the main drag and everywhere you look there is a Nigra scratching his balls. The inevitable Turk who buys and sells everything. He tried to cheat me on every purchase and I spent an hour arguing with this bastard. The Greek shipping agent with his dirty silk shirt and no shoes and his dirty ship that left Esmeraldas seven hours late.

On the boat I talked to a man who knows the Ecuador jungle like his own prick. It seems jungle traders periodically raid the Auca (a tribe of hostile Indians. Shell lost about 20 employees to the Auca in two years) and carry off women they keep penned up for purposes of sex. Sounds interesting. Maybe I could capture an Auca boy.

I have precise instructions for Auca raiding. It's quite simple. You cover both exits of Auca house and shoot everybody you don't wanna fuck.

Arriving in Manta a shabby man in a sweater started opening my bags. I thought he was a brazen thief and gave him a shove. Turns out he was the customs inspector.

The boat gave out with a broken propeller at Las Playas half way between Manta and Guayaquil. I rode ashore on a balsa raft. Arrested on the beach suspect to have floated up from Peru on the Humboldt Current with a young boy and a tooth brush (I travel light, only the essentials) so we are hauled before an old dried up fuck, the withered face of cancerous control. The kid with me don't have paper one. The cops keep saying plaintively:

'But don't you have any papers *at all*?'

I talked us both out in half an hour using the 'We-got-like-two-types-publicity-favorable-and-unfavorable-which-do-you-want?' routine. I am down as writer on tourist card.

*Guayaquil.* Every morning a swelling cry goes up from the kids who sell Luckies in the street—'A ver Luckies,' 'Look here Luckies'—will they still be saying 'A ver Luckies' a hundred years from now? Nightmare fear of stasis. Horror of being finally *stuck* in this place. This fear has followed me all over South America. A horrible sick feeling of final desolation.

'La Asia,' a Chinese restaurant in Guayaquil, looks like 1890 whorehouse opium den. Holes eaten by termites in the floor, dirty tasseled pink lamps. A rotting teak-wood balcony.

Ecuador is really on the skids. Let Peru take over and civilize the place so a man can score for the amenities. I never yet lay a boy in Ecuador and you can't buy any form of junk.

As Ever,

W. Lee

P.S. Met a Pocho cab driver—the Pocho is type found in Mexico who dislikes Mexico and Mexicans. This cab driver told me he was Peruvian but he couldn't stand Peruvians. In Ecuador and Colombia no one will admit anything is wrong with his jerk water country. Like small town citizens in U.S. I recall an army officer in Puerto Leguizamo telling me:

'Ninety percent of the people who come to Colombia never leave.'

He meant, presumably, they were overcome by the charms of the place. I belong to the ten percent who never come back.

As Ever,

Bill

May 12, 1953

Lima

Dear Allen,

I have been looking for what a Waugh character calls 'louche little bistros' with conspicuous success. The bars around the Wholesale Market — Mercado Mayorista — are so full of boys they spill out onto the street, and all wise and available to the Yankee dollar — (one) — never saw anything like it since Vienna in '36. The little bastards steal up a breeze though. Lost a watch and $15 already. The watch didn't run. I never had one that did.

Last night I checked into a hotel with a barefooted Indian to the hilarious amusement of the hotel clerk and his friends (I don't think the average Stateside hotel clerk would be amused at such an occurrence).

Met a boy and went with him to a dance place. Right in the middle of this well lighted non queer dime and dance joint he put his hand on my cock. So I reciprocated and no one paid it any mind. Then he tried to find something worth stealing in my pocket but I had prudently hidden my money in my hat band. All this routine, you understand, is completely good natured and without a trace of violence overt or potential. Finally we cut out together and took a cab and he embraced me and kissed me yet and went to sleep on my shoulder like an affectionate puppy but insisted on getting out at his place.

Now you must understand this is average *non queer* Peruvian boy, a bit juvenile delinquent to be sure. They are the least character armored people I have ever seen. They shit or piss anywhere they feel like it. They have no inhibitions in expressing affection. They climb all over each other and hold hands. If they do go to bed with another male, and they all will

37

for money, they seem to enjoy it. Homosexuality is simply a human potential as is shown by almost unanimous incidence in prisons — and nothing human is foreign or shocking to a South American. I am speaking of the South American at best, a special race part Indian, part white, part God knows what. He is not, as one is apt to think at first fundamentally an Oriental nor does he belong to the West. He is something special unlike anything else. He has been blocked from expression by the Spanish and the Catholic Church. What we need is a new Bolivar who will really get the job done. This is I think what the Colombian Civil War is basically about — the fundamental split between the South American Potential and the Repressive Spanish life-fearing character armadillos. I never felt myself so definitely on one side and unable to see any redeeming features in the other. South America is a mixture of strains all necessary to realize the potential form. They need white blood as they know — Myth of White God — and what did they get but the fucking Spaniards. Still they had the advantage of weakness. Never would have gotten the English out of here. They would have created that atrocity known as a White Man's Country.

South America does not force people to be deviants. You can be queer or a drug addict and still maintain position. Especially if you are educated and well mannered. There is deep respect here for education. In the U.S. you have to be a deviant or exist in dreary boredom. Even a man like Oppenheimer is a deviant tolerated for his usefulness. Make no mistake *all* intellectuals are deviants in U.S.

Extensive Chinatown. I think you could score for junk here. In Colombia and Ecuador nobody ever heard of such a thing. A little weed among coast wise Negroes. Coca, but only in leaf form, among the Indians.

Incidentally you most always see plenty blood in these louche Peruvian bistros. Ramming a broken glass in your opponent's face is standard practice. Everybody does it here.

Love,

Bill

May 23

Lima

Dear Al,

Enclose a routine I dreamed up. The idea did come to me in a dream from which I woke up laughing—

Rolled for $200 in traveler's checks. No loss really as American Express refunds. Recovering from a bout of Pisco neuritis, and Doc has taken a lung x-ray. First Caqueta malaria, then Esmeraldas grippe, now Pisco neuritis— (Pisco is local liquor. Seems to be poison) — can't leave Lima until neuritis clears up.

May 24

*Ho hum dept.* Rolled again. My glasses and a pocket knife. Losing all my fucking valuables in the service.

This is a nation of kleptomaniacs. In all my experience as a homosexual I have never been the victim of such idiotic pilferings of articles no conceivable use to anyone else. Glasses and traveler's checks yet.

Trouble is I share with the late Father Flanagan — he of Boy's Town — the deep conviction that there is no such thing as a bad boy.

39

Got to lay off the juice. Hand shaking so I can hardly write. Must cut short.

Love,
Bill

# ROOSEVELT
# AFTER INAUGURATION

Immediately after the Inauguration Roosevelt appeared on the White House balcony dressed in the purple robes of a Roman Emperor and, leading a blind toothless lion on a gold chain, hog-called his constituents to come and get their appointments. The constituents rushed up grunting and squealing like the hogs they were.

An old queen, known to the Brooklyn Police as "Jerk Off Annie," was named to the Joint Chiefs of Staff, so that the younger staff officers were subject to unspeakable indignities in the lavatories of the Pentagon, to avoid which many set up field latrines in their offices.

To a transvestite Lizzie went the post of Congressional Librarian. She immediately barred the male sex from the premises—a world famous professor of philology suffered a broken jaw at the hands of a bull dyke when he attempted to enter the Library. The Library was given over to Lesbian orgies, which she termed the Rites of the Vested Virgins.

A veteran panhandler was appointed Secretary of State, and disregarding the dignity of his office, solicited nickels and dimes in the corridors of the State Department.

"Subway Slim" the Lush-worker assumed the office of Undersecretary of State and Chief of Protocol, and occasioned diplomatic rupture with England when the English Ambassador "came up on him"—lush-worker term for a lush waking up when you are going through his pockets—at a banquet in the Swedish Embassy.

Lonny the Pimp became Ambassador-at-Large, and went on tour with fifty "secretaries," exercising his despicable trade.

A female impersonator, known as "Eddie the Lady," headed the Atomic Energy Commission, and enrolled the physicists into a male chorus which was booked as "The Atomic Kids."

In short, men who had gone gray and toothless in the faithful service of their country were summarily dismissed in the grossest terms — like: "You're fired you old fuck. Get your piles outa here."—and in many cases thrown bodily out of their offices. Hoodlums and riffraff of the vilest caliber filled the highest offices of the land. To mention only a few of his scandalous appointments:

*Secretary of the Treasury:* "Pantopon Mike," an old-time schmecker.

*Head of the F.B.I.:* A Turkish Bath attendant and specialist in unethical massage.

*Attorney General:* A character known as "The Mink," a peddler of unlicensed condoms and short-con artist.

*Secretary of Agriculture:* "Catfish Luke," the wastrel of Cuntville, Alabama, who had been drunk twenty years on paregoric and lemon extract.

*Ambassador to the Court of St. James's:* "Blubber Wilson," who hustled his goof ball money shaking down fetishists in shoe stores.

*Postmaster General:* "The Yen Pox Kid," an old-time junkie and con man on the skids. Currently working a routine known as "Taking It Off the Eye"—you plant a fake cataract in the savage's eye (savage is con man for sucker) — cheapest trick in the industry.

When the Supreme Court overruled some of the legislation perpetrated by this vile rout, Roosevelt forced that august body, one after the other, on threat of immediate reduction to the rank of Congressional Lavatory Attendants, to submit to intercourse with a purple-assed baboon; so that venerable, honored men surrendered themselves to the embraces of a lecherous snarling simian, while Roosevelt and his strumpet wife and the veteran brown-nose Harry Hopkins, smoking a communal hookah of hashish, watched the lamentable sight with cackles of obscene laughter. Justice Blackstrap succumbed to a rectal hemorrhage on the spot, but Roosevelt only laughed and said coarsely, "Plenty more where that came from."

Hopkins, unable to contain himself, rolled on the floor in sycophantic convulsions, saying over and over, "You're killin' me, Chief. You're killin' me."

Justice Hockactonsvol had both ears bitten off by the simian, and when Chief Justice Howard P. Herringbone asked to be excused, pleading his piles, Roosevelt told him brutally, "Best thing for piles is a baboon's prick up the ass. Right, Harry?"

"Right, Chief. I use no other. All right, H.P. You heard what the man said. Drop your moth eaten ass over that chair and show the visiting simian some Southern hospitality."

Roosevelt then appointed the baboon to replace Justice Blackstrap, "diseased."

"I'll have to remember that one, boss," said Hopkins, breaking into loud guffaws.

So henceforth the proceedings of the Court were carried on with a screeching simian shitting and pissing and masturbating on the table and not infrequently leaping on one of the Justices and tearing him to shreds.

"He is entering a vote of dissent," Roosevelt would say with an evil chuckle.

The vacancies so created were invariably filled by simians, so that, in the course of time, the Supreme Court came to consist of nine purple-assed baboons; and Roosevelt, claiming to be the only one able to interpret their decisions, thus gained control of the highest tribunal in the land.

He then set himself to throw off the restraints imposed by Congress and the Senate. He loosed innumerable crabs and other vermin in both Houses. He had a corps of trained idiots who would rush in at a given signal and shit on the floor, and hecklers equipped with a brass band and fire hoses. He instituted continuous repairs. An army of workmen trooped through the Houses, slapping the solons in the face with boards, spilling hot tar down their necks, dropping tools on their feet, undermining them with air hammers; and finally he caused a steam shovel to be set up on the floors, so that the recalcitrant solons were either buried alive or drowned when the Houses flooded from broken water mains. The survivors attempted to carry on in the street, but were arrested for loitering and sent to the workhouse like common bums. After release they were barred from office on the grounds of their police records.

Then Roosevelt gave himself over to such vile and unrestrained conduct as is shameful to speak of. He instituted a series of contests designed to promulgate the lowest acts and instincts of which the human species is capable. There was a Most Unsavory Act Contest, a Cheapest Trick Contest, Molest a Child Week, Turn in Your Best Friend Week — professional stool pigeons disqualified — and the coveted title of All-Around Vilest Man of the Year. Sample entries: The junkie who stole an opium suppository out of his grandmother's ass; the ship captain who put on women's clothes and rushed into the first lifeboat; the vice-squad cop who framed people for indecent exposure, planting an artificial prick in their fly.

Roosevelt was convulsed with such hate for the human species as it is, that he wished to degrade it beyond recognition. He could endure only the extremes of human behavior. The average, the middle-aged (he viewed middle age as a condition with no relation to chronological age), the middle-class, the bureaucrat filled him with loathing. One of his first acts was to burn every record in Washington; thousands of bureaucrats threw themselves into the flames.

"I'll make the cocksuckers glad to mutate," he would say, looking off into space as if seeking new frontiers of depravity.

June 18
Hotel Touriste
Tingo Maria, Peru

Dear Allen:

Comfortable well-run hotel like a mountain resort. Cool climate. Very high jungle. A group of upper class Peruvians in the hotel. Every few minutes one of them yells, 'Senor *Pinto*' — (he runs the hotel) — this is Latin American humorous routine. Like they look at a dog and yell 'Perro' and everybody laughs.

Talked to a slightly crazed school teacher from California who chewed with her mouth open. The president arrived in Tingo Maria while I was there. Terrible nuisance. No dinner 'til 9 o'clock and I made a scene with the waiter and walked to town and ate a greasy meal.

Stuck here 'til tomorrow on bum steer. I was supposed to see a man about Yage and it turns out he moved away five years ago. This is a farming community with Yugoslav and Italian colonists and a U.S. Point Four Experimental Agriculture Station. As dull a crew of people as I ever saw. Farming towns are awful.

This place gives me the stasis horrors. The feel of *location*, of being just where I am and nowhere else is unendurable. Suppose I should have to live here?

Did you ever read H. G. Wells' *The Country of the Blind*? About a man stuck in a country where all the other inhabitants had been blind so many generations they had lost the concept of sight. He flips.

'But don't you understand? I can *see*.'

As Ever,
Bill

46

July 8
930 Jose Leal, Lima

Dear Allen:

Back in Lima after three day bus ride. Last five days in Pucallpa I was waiting to leave, but trapped by rain and impassible roads and the plane booked solid.

The Naval Lieutenant did a hideous strip tease with his character armor. Everybody yelling, 'For God's sake keep it on.' He began goosing the waiter and when I passed his room in the morning he would rush to the door and show me a hard on and say, 'Hello Bill.' Even the other Peruvians were embarrassed.

The furniture salesman wanted to go in the cocaine business and get rich and live in Lima and drive a fishtail Cadillac. Oh God. People think all they have to do is go in some shady business and they will get rich over night. They don't realize that business shady or legitimate is the same fucking headache. And the old German went on and on about the treasure.

They were driving me crazy with their silly talk and their stupid Spanish jokes. I felt like Ruth amidst the alien corn. When they said that American literature did not exist and English literature was very poor, I lost my temper and told them Spanish literature belonged in the outhouse on a peg with the old Montgomery Ward catalogues. I was shaking with rage and realized how the place was dragging me.

Met a young Dane and took Yage with him. He immediately vomited it up and avoided me after that—he evidently thought I had tried to poison him and he was saved only by the prompt reaction of his hygienic Scandinavian gut. I never knew a Dane that wasn't bone dull.

Terrible bus trip back to Tingo Maria where I got drunk and was helped to bed by the cutest assistant truck driver.

Hung up two days in Huanuco. An awful dump. Spent my time wandering around taking pictures trying to get the bare dry mountains, the wind in the dusty poplar trees, the little parks with statues of generals and cupids, and Indians lolling about with a special South American abandon, chewing coca — the government sells it in controlled shops — and doing absolutely nothing. At 5 o'clock had a few drinks in a Chinese restaurant, where the owner picked his teeth and went over his books. How sane they are and how little they expect from life. He looked like junk to me but you can never be sure with the Chinese. They are all basically junkies in outlook. A lunatic came in the bar and went into a long incomprehensible routine. He had the figure $17,000,000 written on the back of his shirt and turned around to show it to me. Then he went over and harangued the owner. The owner sat there picking his teeth. He showed neither contempt nor amusement nor sympathy. He just sat there picking a molar and occasionally taking the toothpick out and looking at the end of it.

Passed through some of the highest towns in the world. They have a curious exotic Mongolian or Tibetan look. Horribly cold.

Three times 'all the foreigners' were asked to get out of the bus and register with the police: passport number, age, profession. All this pure formality. No trace of suspicion or interrogation. What do they do with these records? Use them for toilet paper I expect.

Lima cold damp and depressing. Went to the Mercado. None of the boys around any more. Bum kick to go in a bar I used to like, nobody there I know or want to know, the bar has been moved for no organic

48

reason from one side of the joint to the other — different waiters, nothing I want to hear on the juke box — (am I in the right bar?) — everybody has gone and I am alone in a nowhere place. Every night the people will be uglier and stupider, the fixtures more hideous, the waiters ruder, the music more grating on and on like a speedup movie into a nightmare vortex of mechanical disintegration and meaningless change.

I did see one boy in the Mercado I knew before I left Lima. He looked *years older* (I had been away six weeks). When I first saw him he wouldn't drink, saying with a shy smile:

'I am still a boy.'

Now he was drunk. Scar under left eye. I touched it and said, 'Knife?'

He said, 'Yes' and smiled, his eyes glazed and bloodshot.

Suddenly I wanted to leave Lima right away. This feeling of urgency has followed me like my ass all over South America. I have to be somewhere at a certain time (in Guayaquil I dragged the Peruvian consul out of his house after office hours so I could get a visa and leave a day earlier).

Where am I going in such a hurry? Appointment in Talara, Tingo Maria, Pucallpa, Panama, Guatemala, Mexico City? I don't know. Suddenly I have to leave right now.

Love,
Bill

July 10, 1953

Lima

Dear Allen,

Last night I took last of Yage mixture I brought back from Pucallpa. No use transporting to U.S. It doesn't keep more than a few days. This morning, still high. This is what occurred to me:

Yage is space time travel. The room seems to shake and vibrate with motion. The blood and substance of many races, Negro, Polynesian, Mountain Mongol, Desert Nomad, Polyglot Near East, Indian — new races as yet unconceived and unborn, combinations not yet realized passes through your body. Migrations, incredible journeys through deserts and jungles and mountains (stasis and death in closed mountain valleys where plants sprout out of your cock and vast crustaceans hatch inside and break the shell of the body), across the Pacific in an outrigger canoe to Easter Island. The Composite City where all human potentials are spread out in a vast silent market.

Minarets, palms, mountains, jungle. A sluggish river jumping with vicious fish, vast weed grown parks where boys lie in the grass or play cryptic games. Not a locked door in the City. Anyone comes in your room any time. The Chief of Police is a Chinese who picks his teeth and listens to denunciations presented by a lunatic. Every now and then the Chinese takes the tooth pick out of his mouth and looks at the end of it. Hipsters with smooth copper colored faces lounge in doorways twisting shrunk heads on gold chains, their faces blank with an insect's unseeing calm.

Behind them, through the open door, tables and booths, and bars and rooms and kitchens and baths, copulating couples on rows of brass beds, criss cross of a thousand hammocks, junkies tying up, opium smokers, hashish smokers, people eating, talking, bathing, shitting back into a haze of smoke and steam.

Gaming tables where the games are played for incredible stakes. From time to time a player leaps up with a despairing inhuman cry having lost his youth to an old man or become Latah to his opponent. But there are higher stakes than youth or Latah. Games where only two players in the world know what the stakes are.

All houses in the City are joined. Houses of sod with high mountain Mongols blinking in smoky doorways, houses of bamboo and teak wood, houses of adobe, stone, and red brick, South Pacific and Maori houses, houses in trees and houses on river boats, wood houses 100 feet long sheltering entire tribes, houses of old boxes and corrugated iron where old men sit in rotting rags talking to themselves and cooking down Canned Heat, great rusty iron racks rising 200 feet in the air from swamps and rubbish with perilous partitions built on multileveled platforms and hammocks swinging over the void.

Expeditions leave for unknown places with unknown purpose. Strangers arrive on rafts of old packing crates tied together with rotten rope, they stagger in out of the jungle their eyes swollen shut by insect bites, they come down the mountain trail on cracked, bleeding feet through the dusty, windy outskirts of the City where people shit in rows along adobe walls and vultures fight over fish heads, they drop down into the parks in patched parachutes. They are escorted by a drunken cop to register in a vast public lavatory. The data taken down is put on pegs and used as toilet paper.

The cooking smells of all countries hang over the City, a haze of opium, hashish, and the resinous red smoke of cooking Yage, smell of the jungle and salt water and the rotting river and dried excrement and sweat and genitals. High mountain flutes and jazz and bebop and one stringed Mongol instruments and Gypsy xylophones and Arabian bag pipes.

The City is visited by epidemics of violence and the untended dead are eaten by vultures in the street. Funerals and cemeteries are not permitted. Albinos blink in the sun, boys sit in trees languidly masturbating, people eaten by unknown diseases spit at passersby and bite them and throw pus and scabs and assorted vectors (insects suspected of carrying a disease) hoping to infect somebody.

Whenever you get blackout drunk you wake up with one of these diseased faceless citizens in your bed who has spent all night exhausting his ingenuity trying to infect you. But no one knows how the diseases are transmitted or indeed if they are contagious. These diseased beggars live in a maze of burrows under the City and pop out anywhere often pushing up through the floor of a crowded cafe.

Followers of obsolete unthinkable trades doodling in Etruscan, addicts of drugs not yet synthesized, pushers of souped-up Harmine, junk reduced to pure habit offering precarious vegetable serenity, liquids to induce Latah, cut antibiotics, Tithonian longevity serum; black marketeers of World War III, pitchmen selling remedies for radiation sickness, investigators of infractions denounced by bland paranoid chess players, servers of fragmentary warrants charging unspeakable mutilations of the spirit taken down in hebephrenic shorthand, bureaucrats of spectral departments, officials of unconstituted police states; a Lesbian dwarf who has perfected operation Bang-utot, the lung erection that strangles a sleeping enemy; sellers of orgone tanks and relaxing machines, brokers of exquisite dreams and memories tested on the sensitized cells of junk sickness and bartered for the raw materials of the will; doctors skilled in treatment of diseases dormant in the black dust of ruined cities, gathering virulence in the white blood of eyeless worms feeling slowly to the surface and the human hosts, maladies of the ocean floor and the stratosphere, maladies of the laboratory and atomic war, excisors of telepathic sensitivity, osteopaths of the spirit.

A place where the unknown past and the emergent future meet in a vibrating soundless hum. Larval entities waiting for a live one.

William Lee

**SEVEN YEARS LATER (1960)**

June 10, 1960

Estafeta Correo

Pucallpa, Peru

Dear Bill:

I'm still in Pucallpa—ran into a little plump fellow, Ramon Penadillo — who'd been friend to Robert Frank (photographer of our movie) in '46 or so here. Ramon took me to his Curandero — in whom he has a lot of faith and about whose supernatural curing powers he talks a lot, too much, about— The Maestro, as he's called, being a very mild and simple seeming cat of 38 or so — who prepared a drink for 3 of us the other night; and then last night I attended a regular curing all nite drinking session with about 30 other men and women in a hut in jungly outskirts of Pucallpa behind the gaswork field.

The first time, much stronger than the drink I had in Lima. Ayahuasca can be bottled and transported and stay strong, as long as it does not ferment— needs well closed bottle. Drank a cup — slightly old mix, several days old and slightly fermented also—lay back and after an hour (in bamboo hut outside his shack, where he cooks) — began seeing or feeling what I thought was the Great Being, or some sense of It, approaching my mind like a big wet vagina — lay back in that for a while — only image I can come up with is of a big black hole of God-Nose thru which I peered into a mystery—and the black hole surrounded by all creation — particularly colored snakes—all real.

I felt somewhat like what this image represents, the sense of it so real.

The eye is imaginary image, to give life to the picture. Also a great feeling of pleasantness in my body, no nausea. Lasted in different phases about

57

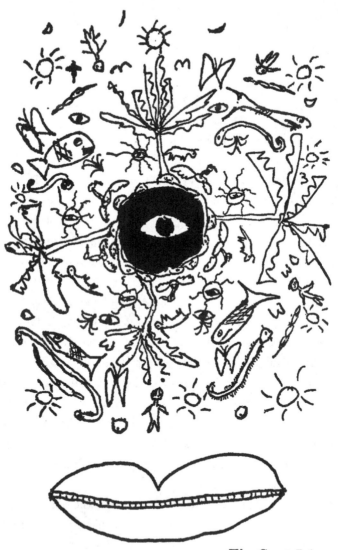

*The Great Being*

2 hours—the effects wore off after 3—the phantasy itself lasted from ¾ of hour after I drank to 2½ hours later more or less.

---

There is a branch of the Schweitzer Hospital here with a German Dr. Binder in charge, visited him to cure my warts, still there, he studied Ayahuasca and gave me Schultes' report (Harvard Botanical Series 1957—identification of the plants — I'll add info on this later) — also recommended me Paococha village down river 6 hours, he knows the chief of — I got hammock and mosquito net and will visit Ayahuasquero there next week.

---

Went back and talked to the Maestro, gave him 35 soles ($1.50) for services and talked with him about peyote and LSD—he'd heard of peyote — he's a mestizo who studied in San Martin (upper Huallaga territory)—he gave me samples of his mix—uses young cultivated Ayahuasca plant in his back yard, and mixes that about half and half with a catalyst known as the 'Mescla' which is another leaf known in Chama Indian language as Cahua (pron Coura) and locally by him in Pucallpa is called Chacruna. Said he'd get me more samples to bring back to Lima Natural History Museum to identify. Cooks the mixes together all day and strains the broth, gives the drained leaves a second cook too. Anyway the preparation is not excessively secret — I think Schultes saw and knows the preparation. Can add other leaves of other plants too, I don't know these combinations and effects yet. I also gave the Maestro a tube of codeineetas to try out—he seemed generally interested in drugs—sincere—and

59

not mercenary at all — good type — has quite a following here — does physical cures, his specialty.

Anyway to make long story short, went back to formal group session in huts last night — this time the brew was prepared fresh and presented with full ceremony — he crooning (and blowing cigarette or pipe smoke) tenderly over the cupmouth for several minutes before — (enamel cup, I remember your plastic cup) — then I light cigarette, blow a puff of smoke over cup, and drain. Saw a shooting star — Aerolito — before going in, and full moon, and he served me up first — then lay down expecting God knows what other pleasant vision and then I began to get high — and then the whole fucking Cosmos broke loose around me, I think the strongest and worst I've ever had it nearly — (I still reserve the Harlem experiences, being Natural, in abeyance. The LSD was Perfection but didn't get me so deep in nor so horribly in) — First I began to realize my worry about the mosquitoes or vomiting was silly as there was the great stake of Life and Death — I felt faced by Death, my skull in my beard on pallet on porch rolling back and forth and settling finally as if in reproduction of the last physical move I make before settling into real death — got nauseous, rushed out and began vomiting, all covered with snakes, like a Snake Seraph, colored serpents in aureole all around my body, I felt like a snake vomiting out the universe — or a Jivaro in head-dress with fangs vomiting up in realization of the Murder of the Universe — my death to come — everyone's death to come — all unready — I unready — all around me in the trees the noise of these spectral animals the other Drinkers vomiting (normal part of the cure sessions) in the night in their awful solitude in the universe — vomiting up their will to live, be preserved in this body, almost — Went back and lay down — Ramon came over quite

*The Vomiter*

tender and nurse-like (he hadn't drunk, he's sort of an aide to help the sufferers) asked me if I was OK and 'Bien Mareado' (Good and drunk?) — I said 'Bastante' and went back to listen to the spectre that was approaching my mind — The whole hut seemed rayed with spectral presences all suffering transfiguration with contact with a single mysterious Thing that was our fate and was sooner or later going to kill us — the Curandero crooning, keeping up a very tender, repeated and then changing simple tune, comfort sort of, God knows what signified — seemed to signify some point of reference I was unable to contact yet — I was frightened and simply lay there with wave after wave of death-fear, fright, rolling over me till I could hardly stand it, didn't want to take refuge in rejecting it as Illusion, for it was too real and too familiar — especially as if in rehearsal of Last Minute Death my head rolling back and forth on the blanket and finally settling in last position of stillness and hopeless resignation to God knows what Fate — for my being — felt completely lost strayed soul — outside of contact with some Thing that seemed present — finally had a sense that I might face the Question there and then, and choose to die and understand — and leave my body to be found in the morning — I guess grieving everybody — couldn't bear and leave Peter and my father so alone — afraid to die yet then and so never took the chance (if there was a chance, perhaps somehow there was) — also as if everybody in session in central radiotelepathic contact with the same problem — the Great Being within ourselves — Coming back from vomit saw a man knees to chest I thought I saw as X ray his skull and realized he was crouched there as in shroud (with towel mosquito protection wrapped round his face) suffering the same Woe and separation — Thought of people, saw their images clearly, you — mysterious apparently know more than I do now and why don't you communicate, or can't you, or have I ignored it? Lucien seemingly an angel in his annihilation of vanity and giving forth new life in children — 'If any interplanetary news comes thru' he said 'I'll be the first to be relaying it on the wires in a way that won't get it fucked up' — Francesca his wife — sort of a Seraph of Woman, all women (as all men) the same — spectral creatures put here mysteriously to live, be the living Gods, and suffer Crucifixion of death like Christ, but either get lost and die in soul or get in contact and give new birth to continue the Process of Being (tho' they themselves die, or do they?) — and I lost and poor Peter who depends on me for some Heaven I haven't got, lost — and I keep rejecting women, who come to minister to me — decided to have children somehow, a resolution in the hallucination — but the suffering was about as much as I could bear and the thought of more suffering even deeper to come made me despair — felt, still feel, like lost soul, surrounded by ministering angels (Ramon, the Maestro, yourself, the whole common world of Diers) — and my poor mother died in God knows what state of suffering — I can't stand it — vomited again (Ramon had come over and told me to vomit off the porch where I was lying, if I had to later — very careful kind situation) I mean, is this a good group — I remember your saying watch out *whose* vision you get — but God knows I don't know who to turn to finally when the chips are down spiritually and I have to depend on my own Serpent-self's memory of merry visions of Blake — or depend on nothing and enter anew — but enter what? — Death? — and at that moment — vomiting still feeling like a Great lost Serpent-seraph vomiting in consciousness of the Transfiguration to come — with the Radiotelepathy sense of a Being whose presence I had not yet fully sensed—too Horrible for me, still — to accept the fact of total communication with say everyone an eternal seraph male and female at once — and me a lost soul seeking help — well slowly the intensity began to fade, I being incapable of moving in any direction spiritually — not knowing who to look to or what to look for — not quite trusting to ask the Maestro — tho' in the Vision of the scene it was he who was the local logical Ministering Spirit to trust, if anyone — went over and sat by him (as Ramon gently suggested) to be 'blown' — that is he croons a song to you to cure your soul and blows smoke at you — rather a comforting presence — tho' by now the steep fear had passed — that being over got up and took my piece of cloth I brought against mosquitoes and went home in moonlight with plump Ramon — who said the more you saturate yourself with Ayahuasca the deeper you go — visit the moon, see the dead, see God — see Tree Spirits — etc.

I hardly have the nerve to go back, afraid of some real madness, a Changed Universe permanently changed — tho' I guess change it must for me someday — much less as planned before, go up the river six hours to drink with an Indian tribe Dr. Binder says are OK — I suppose I will — meanwhile will wait here another week in Pucallpa and drink a few more times with same group — I wish I knew who, if anyone, there is to work with that *knows*, if anyone knows, who I am or what I am. I wish I could hear from you. I think I'll be here long enough for a letter to reach me — write

Allen Ginsberg

---

If I do leave here before 2 weeks and letter arrives it will be forwarded to me promptly in Lima so I'll hear from you there but I do want to hear from you Bill so please write and advise me whatever you can if you can. I don't know if I'm going mad or not and it's difficult to face more—tho' I suppose I will and be able to protect myself by treating *that* consciousness as a temporary illusion and return to temporary Normal consciousness when the effects wear off— (I begin to glimpse the call of Haitian voodoo) — but this almost schizophrenic alteration of consciousness is fearful—and also the sense of not knowing who, personally, around me to open up to. I had arrangements to bring some back to NY but am almost afraid to—I'm no Curandero, I'm lost myself, and afraid of giving a nightmare I can't stop to others like Peter.

I don't know how all this sounds to you but you know me reasonably well so write, fast, please.

Everything is OK, I suppose, in case this all just worries you unnecessarily, I'll be alright—

Love,

Allen

P.S. The last horror, in bookstore this morning buying this pen, heard old nostalgic Nelson Eddy record of 'Maytime' I used to cry over in childhood and it was like a reminder of Death, so sad — 'will you love me ever?'

Extra added Attraction—some excerpts from Ether notes I took 2 weeks ago in Lima, in a minor key.

Aether—

      The ringing sound in all the senses
         of everything that has ever been Created
         all the combinations recurring over and
            over again as before—

     Every possible Combination of Being—all
         the old ones:—all the old Hindu,
        Sabahadabadie-pluralic universes
        ringing in Grandiloquent
              Bearded Juxtaposition
        with all their minarets and moonlit
             towers enlaced with iron
                or porcelain embroidery,
       all have existed—
             and the Sages with
       white hair who sat crosslegged on
           a female couch—
       hearkening to whatever music came
            from out the wood or street,
       whatever bird that whistled in the marketplace
       whatever note the clock struck to say
            Time—
       whatever drug, or aire, they breathed
         to make them think so deep
            or hear so simply what
              had passed

like a car passing in the 1960 street
    beside the Governmental Palace
        in Peru, this Lima,
    in the year I write —


    A Buddha as of old, with the sirens of
whatever machinery making ringing noises in
        the street.
And streetlight reflected in the RR station
        front facade window in a
         dinky port in Backwash
  of the murky forgotten
        fabulous whatever
         Civilization of
          Eternity :—
with the RR station clock ring midnight,
    as of now,
      & waiting for the 6th,
      to write a word,
and end on the last chime — remember
    This *one* twelve was struck
      before
and never again; both.


and I turn back from the balcony where I stood
      looking at the Cross (afraid)
      and stars

thinking of the BONG of midnight —
    Sages of Asia, or the white beards in Persia,
        Scribbling on the margins of their scrolls
          in delicate ink
remembering with tears the ancient clockbells of their
              cities
and the cities that had been — and
        Affirm with laughing eyes —
the world is as we see it,
    male and female, passing
as it passes thru the years,
        as has before & will, perhaps
    with all its countless pearls
And all the bloody noses of Eternity —
          and all the old mistakes —
          Including
this old consciousness, which has seen
itself before — (thus the locust-whistle
of antiquity's nightwatch in my eardrum)


           I'm scribbling
nothings,
page upon page of profoundest
        nothing,
as scribed the Ancient Hebe, when
        he wrote Adonoi or One —
all to amuse or make money or deceive —

O BELL TIME, RING THY
MIDNIGHT FOR THE BILLIONTH
SOUNDY TIME, I HEAR AGAIN!

June 21     1960     Present Time     Pre- Sent Time
Cargo American Express
  London                      England

Dear Allen:

There is no thing to fear. Vaya adelante. Look. Listen. Hear. Your AYUASKA consciousness is more valid than 'Normal Consciousness'? Whose 'Normal Consciousness'? Why return to? Why are you surprised to see me? You are following in my steps. I know thee way. And yes know the area better than you I think. Tried more than once to tell you to communicate what I know. You did not or could not listen. 'You can not show to anyone what he has not seen.' Brion Gysin For Hassan Sabbah. Listen now? Take the enclosed copy of this letter. Cut along the lines. Rearrange putting section one by section three and section two by section four. Now read aloud and you will hear My Voice. Whose voice? Listen. Cut and rearrange in any combination. Read aloud. I can not choose but hear. Don't think about it. Don't theorize. Try it. Do the same with your poems. With any poems any prose. Try it. You want 'Help'. Here it is. Pick it up on it. And always remember. 'Nothing Is True. Everything is permitted' Last Words of Hassan Sabbah The Old Man Of The Mountain. LISTEN TO MY LAST WORDS ANY WORLD. LISTEN ALL YOU BOARDS SYNDICATES AND GOVERNMENTS OF THE EARTH. AND YOU POWER POWERS BEHIND WHAT FILTH DEALS CONSUMMATED IN WHAT LAVATORY TO TAKE WHAT IS NOT YOURS. TO SELL THE GROUND FROM UNBORN FEET. LISTEN. WHAT I HAVE TO SAY IS FOR ALL MEN EVERY-

WHERE. I REPEAT FOR ALL. NO ONE IS EXCLUDED. FREE TO
ALL WHO PAY. FREE TO ALL WHO PAIN PAY.
WHAT SCARED YOU ALL INTO TIME? WHAT SCARED YOU
ALL INTO YOUR BODIES? INTO SHIT FOREVER? DO YOU
WANT TO STAY THERE FOREVER? THEN LISTEN TO THE
LAST WORDS OF HASSAN SABBAH. LISTEN LOOK OR SHIT
FOREVER. LISTEN LOOK OR SHIT FOREVER. WHAT SCARED
YOU INTO TIME? INTO BODY? INTO SHIT? I WILL TELL YOU.
THE WORD. THE-THEE WORD. IN THEE BEGINNING WAS THE
WORD. SCARED YOU ALL INTO SHIT FOREVER. COME OUT
FOREVER. COME OUT OF THE TIME WORD THE FOREVER.
COME OUT OF THE BODY WORD THEE FOREVER. COME
OUT OF THE SHIT WORD THE FOREVER. ALL OUT OF TIME
AND INTO SPACE. FOREVER. THERE IS NO THING TO FEAR.
THERE IS NO THING IN SPACE. THAT IS ALL ALL ALL HASSAN
SABBAH. THERE IS NO WORD TO FEAR. THERE IS NO WORD.
THAT IS ALL ALL ALL HASSAN SABBAH. IF YOU I CANCEL ALL
YOUR WORDS FOREVER. AND THE WORDS OF HASSAN SAB-
BAH I AS ALSO CANCEL. ACROSS ALL YOUR SKIES SEE THE
SILENT WRITING OF BRION GYSIN HASSAN SABBAH. THE
WRITING OF SPACE. THE WRITING OF SILENCE.

LOOK      LOOK      LOOK

AMIGOS MUCHACHOS A TRAVES DE TODOS SUS CIELOS
VEA LA ESCRITURA SILENCIOSA DE BRION GYSIN HASSAN
SABBAH. LA ESCRITURA DE SILENCIO LA ESCRITURA DE

ESPACIO. ESO ES TODO TODO TODO HASSAN SABBAH

VEA        VEA        VEA

When will you return — ? The Cut Up Method is explained in MIN-
UTES TO GO. Which is already out in the States. I will send you a copy
but where to? George Whitman says to look up his old friend Silvester
de Castro in Panama City. Connected with the municipal symphony and
the University. Hasta Al Vista Amigo.

> Best
>
> William Burroughs
> For Hassan Sabbah
> *Fore! Hassan Sabbah*

PS. NO ONE IN HIS SENSES WOULD TRUST 'THE UNIVERSE'.
SWEPT WITH CON THE MILLIONS STOOD UNDER THE
SIGNS. WHO EVER PAID OFF A MARK A GOOK AN APE A
HUMAN ANIMAL? NO BODY EXCEPT HASSAN SABBAH

# EPILOGUE (1963)

San Francisco
August 28, 1963

To whom it may concern:

Self deciphers this correspondence thus: the vision of ministering angels my fellow man and woman first wholly glimpsed while the Curandero gently crooned human in Ayahuasca trance-state 1960 was prophetic of transfiguration of self consciousness from homeless mind sensation of eternal fright to incarnate body feeling present bliss now actualized 1963.

Old love, as ever
Allen Ginsberg

# I AM DYING, MEESTER?

Panama clung to our bodies — Probably cut — Anything made this dream — It has consumed the customers of fossil orgasm — Ran into my old friend Jones — So badly off, forgotten, coughing in 1920 movie — Vaudeville voices hustle sick dawn breath on bed service — Idiot Mambo spattered backwards — I nearly suffocated trying on the boy's breath — That's Panama — Nitrous flesh swept out by your voice and end of receiving set — Brain eating birds patrol the low frequency brain waves — Post card waiting forgotten civilians 'and they are all on jelly fish, Meester — Panama photo town — Dead post card of junk.'

Sad hand down backward time track — Genital pawn ticket peeled his stale underwear — Brief boy on screen laughing my skivvies all the way down — Whispers of dark street in Puerto Assis — Meester smiles through the village wastrel — Orgasm siphoned back telegram: 'Johnny pants down.' — (That stale summer dawn smell in the garage — Vines twisting through steel — Bare feet in dog's excrement.)

Panama clung to our bodies from Las Palmas to David on camphor sweet smells of cooking paregoric — Burned down the republic — The druggist no glot clom Fliday — Panama mirrors of 1910 under seal in any drug store — He threw in the towel, morning light on cold coffee —

Junk kept nagging me: 'Lushed in East St. Louis, I *knew* you'd come scraping bone — Once a junky always spongy and rotten — I *knew* your life — Junk sick four days there.'

Stale breakfast table — Little cat smile — Pain and death smell of his sickness in the room with me — Three souvenir shots of Panama city —

Old friend came and stayed all day — Face eaten by 'I need *more*' — I have noticed this in the New World — 'You come with me, Meester?'

And Joselito moved in at Las Playas during the essentials — Stuck in this place — Iridescent lagoons, swamp delta, gas flares — Bubbles of coal gas still be saying 'A ver, Luckees!' a hundred years from now — A rotting teak wood balcony propped up by Ecuador.

'The brujo began crooning a special case — It was like going under ether into the eyes of a shrunken head — Numb, covered with layers of cotton — Don't know if you got my last hints trying to break out of this numb dizziness with Chinese characters — All I want is out of here — Hurry up please — Took possession of me — How many plots have made a botanical expedition like this before they could take place? — Scenic railways — I am dying cross wine dizziness — I was saying over and over "shifted commissions where the awning flaps" Flashes in front of my eyes your voice and end of the line.'

That whining Panama clung to our bodies — I went into Chico's Bar on mouldy pawn ticket, waiting in 1920 movie for a rum coke — Nitrous flesh under this honky tonk swept out by your voice: 'Driving Nails In My Coffin' — Brain eating birds patrol 'Your Cheating Heart' — Dead post card waiting a place forgotten — Light concussion of 1920 movie — Casual adolescent had undergone special G.I. processing — Evening on the boy's flesh naked — Kept trying to touch in sleep — 'Old photographer trick wait for Johnny — Here goes Mexican cemetery.' On the sea wall met a boy with red and white striped T shirt — P.G. town in the purple twilight — The boy peeled off his stale underwear scraping erection — Warm rain on the iron roof — Under the ceiling fan stood naked on bed service — Bodies touched electric film, contact sparks tingled — Fan whiffs of young hard on washing adolescent T shirt — The blood smells drowned voices and end of the line — That's Panama — Sad movie drifting in islands of rubbish, black lagoons and fish people waiting a place forgotten — Fossil honky tonk swept out by a ceiling fan — Old photographer trick tuned them out.

'I am dying, Meester?'

Flashes in front of my eyes naked and sullen — Rotten dawn wind in sleep — Death rot on Panama photo where the awning flaps.

*William Burroughs*

# APPENDICES

# Appendix 1

## From Burroughs' June 1953 "Yage" manuscript

Inquiring in the environs of Puerto Leguizamo I found the use of Yage widespread among both Indians and whites. Most everybody grows it in their back yard. The method of preparation is boiling.

After a week in Leguizamo I took a plane back to Bogota. I found no money waiting for me there — it seems my check was stolen from the mail. For a week I was flat broke and reduced to the shoddy expedient of stealing my drinking alcohol from the University Laboratory placed at the disposal of the visiting scientist. The extraction of Yage alkaloids is a relatively simple process. The principal alkaloid — Yageina — is a brown feathery powder. It takes about 4 pounds of vine to extract ½ gram of the pure stuff. The Putumayo dose is about one gram of Yageina or half the lethal dose for the average adult. Half the lethal dose of any drug doesn't leave much margin for individual susceptibility. A grain and a half of morphine would kill an appreciable percent of patients.

My experiments with pure Yage were not conclusive. I never got blue flashes or any pronounced sharpening of mental imagery. I did however notice aphrodisiac effects.

*Revised in light of subsequent experience. Addition of other leaves which I have identified as Palicourea Sp. Rubiaceae is* <u>essential</u> *for full hallucinating effect. Revised*

When I started looking for Yage I was thinking along the line the medicine men have secrets the whites don't know about. Most of these secrets turn out to be a con the Brujo puts down on the public so he can preserve a semblance of monopoly and everybody won't start brewing up the same mess in his own pot. Every Indian and most whites in the Amazon region from Colombia to Bolivia and on out to the Atlantic knows the Yage vine. The Brujos say they are the only ones competent to prepare it, two other secret plants must be cooked in the mixture, the Brujo has to croon over it and spit in it and shake a whisk broom over it otherwise the Yage is nowhere. And if a woman catches even a glimpse of these proceedings the Yage curdles on the spot and turns poison[ous].

The fact is Yage is Yage and anyone can prepare it in an hour or so if he has enough of the Yage vine. It takes a surprising amount to make a dose for one person. About four pounds of the whole vine or a large double hand full of the shaved bark. There are two methods of preparing it for use. The method used by the Kofans of the Putumayo — the Kofans are the acknowledged Yage artists — is to pound about 4 pounds of whole vine per person, cook the pulped wood all day adding just enough water to cover. The final result is 2 ounces more or less of black oily liquid. This is a dangerously strong dose — half the lethal dose — but it is standard in that area and it would not occur to them to take less or to take this amount slowly. Indians are like that. They have a set way of doing things which they consider of its nature immutable.

The other method of preparation uses only the bark — the inner bark is supposed to be most active. The bark is shaved off the vine with a knife and immediately turns red on exposure to air. You need to scrape about 4 pieces of vine each 8 or 10 inches long to have enough bark for one person. The bark is soaked in cold water a few hours, the water strained off and taken over a period of an hour. I estimate this method to provide about one third the dose you get with two ounces of the boiled mixture. Also the larger volume and slower administration cushions the effect. I never experience anxiety or hallucinations from this amount of Yage.

To summarize: Yage is a fast growing vine with distribution throughout Amazon region and I understand on the coastal regions of Ecuador as well. I have not confirmed this, and one cardinal rule for orientation in South America is don't believe anything until you see it. The vine grows to length of 40 feet or more and attains diameter of three to four inches.

The effect of Yage is weed. I would not classify it as a new narcotic. However Yage has special features: The effect varies qualitatively with the dosage. Take $\frac{1}{8}$ grain of morphine you will feel a slight but perceptible junk kick. Take $\frac{1}{4}$ liter of Yage infusion and you feel nothing. Take the full liter you feel weed effect with blue flashes, chills, some nausea and loss of coordination. Take the boiled preparation standard dose and you experience paranoid delusions and hallucinations, horrible nausea, chills and a complete loss of coordination. I am sure that this dose would kill anyone in poor condition. About two months before I arrived a man died outside Mocoa on this dose of Yage.

I can not say whether Yage increases the telepathic faculties. Everyone white and Indian in the area firmly believes this. "So there we were" they say "High on Yage laying around in a telepathic state." Any drug used in common with others conveys mutual empathy. I don't have [to] ask someone or speak his language to know when he is junk sick and exactly how it feels.

*Complete tolerance is rapidly acquired. They do not get sick.*

83

# Appendix 2

## Burroughs' letter to Ginsberg, July 9, 1953

[July 9, 1953
Lima]

Dear Allen,

Few additions on diseased beggars in The City.

"Beggars eaten with unknown diseases leap on the passerby and attempt to sodomize him in the street, throw pus, and scabs, and assorted vectors—insects suspected of conveying a disease—pop out festered eyes with great force and accuracy, all this in the hope of infecting someone . . .

One ingenious Leper solicits alms by coating his rotting feet with honey and sitting on an ant hill for a certain period each day, figuring the spreading numbness will outdistance the ants until he has no more to give his public. Others give themselves enemas of hot acid on street corners, or break off dried, black fingers and genitals to sell as souvenirs. One notable beggar has such a foul breath he has been known to cause death by nausea. He has only to ~~open his mouth~~ part his lips and hiss threateningly and the passerby empties his pockets. These diseased beggars live in a maze of burrows under the city and pop out anywhere often pushing up through the floor of a crowded cafe.

The most dreaded disease is known as The Crusts. A vast crab or centipede hatches out inside the body and finally cracks through. Inasmuch as the place where breakthrough occurs is quarantined, and the occupants compelled to dispose of the Stranger as best they can, a man 8 months gone with centipede can name his own price to go somewhere else. Besides which, the terminal stages, when the centipede can be seen stirring beneath the skin, are so abjectly repulsive, impose such blighting knowledge, that few recover from witnessing this spectacle. They succumb to a creeping apathy, ~~too much trouble to~~ and die of inertia."

I feel like I just saw a centipede hatch. Tired, inert. Appalled by prospect of packing etc. A mysterious plague has broke[n] out just where I have to pass through in the north of the country. People dying like flies. No one has any idea what it is, or how conveyed. Sounds like some virulent form of polio or meningitis. 100 people up there are in deep coma and about 25 dead in last few days. See you soon,

As Ever,

Willy Lee

*Bill*

## Appendix 3

## From Burroughs' December 1953 "Yage" manuscript

*May 24* [1953]
*Lima*

Dear Jean,

Sitting around waiting for my neuritis to clear up. Such a bore. I guess nobody can hit this rotten lush month after month.

Connected for Yage. The Putumayo, under misapprehension I was Texas Oil incognito, rolled out the carpet: eating in officers' mess, sleeping in the governor's house, free chow, free boat rides, free plane rides.

Yage is prevalent throughout the area and you can score anywhere. What a shit Cotter was. I could score in the headwaters of the Baboons-asshole in ten minutes. He's the kind of citizen it hurts him deep down inside to do anything for anybody.

First time I took Yage the witch doctor slipped me an overdose and I came near going in convulsions way out in the brush with nobody but this old drunken fuck of a witch doctor. If I hadn't had some nembutals would likely have left my mortal remains in the Putumayo. An overdose of Yage is horrible experience. Delirium, hallucinations and wracking nausea. In smaller doses effect is similar to weed. Telepathy? Everyone, white and Indian believes this.

"So there we were" they say "High on Yage, lying around in a telepathic state."

Fact is Amazon Basin is infested with bull shit. One cardinal rule for orienting yourself in the area is don't believe a thing you hear just wait 'til you see. Take it from an old bushwhacker, my dear. For example a Peruvian Major, stationed on the Putumayo, told me as a fact there are Anacondas 75 feet long in the jungle — I doubt if Anacondas ever grow more than 30 feet. Such a beast (75 feet long) would die of starvation. You know the food situation in the area. Met a reporter from *Exposure* in Putumayo.

The whole Amazon area has too many people in it. No trick, by the way, to go down Amazon to the Atlantic. Steam boat service. The best people in South America are the Indians. Only boy I went to bed with didn't steal something on the way out was an Indian. My next expedition is going to include all tribes known to practice homosexuality. Need a live one to put up the $.

Please write. Haven't heard from you in 5 months.

As Ever.


P.S. Liberals vs Conservatives. The Conservatives are ugly looking shits. All the good looking kids and all the Indians are Liberals. Needless to say so am I. Going to have a quick look at the Peru jungle.

## Appendix 4

## From Burroughs' January 1956 "*Yagé* Article" manuscript

*Jan 3, 56 received*

*Beginning (II)*

### *YAGÉ*
### *DRAFT OF ARTICLE*

"Yes in the Putumayo are many strange things."

I checked an impatient question. I was learning the South American way of letting things take their course. The Latin American *mañana* does not mean necessarily pointless delay and laziness. It means wait until the time is right.

I had reconciled myself to the South American practice of saving the important question until you are getting up to leave, and then with: "Oh, and by the way . . ." you come to the point of your visit. Why not? It is courteous not to force your own necessities on someone else, but to introduce them modestly after an interchange of conversation which may have turned up something you have to offer the other.

My host was a German, but thirty years in South America . . . It was best to proceed in the South American way, which I found congenial to my temperament.

The room was lined with books and comfortably warmed by two electric heaters, the first heat I had seen in Colombia. The man opposite me was wearing a worn dressing gown of blue silk. He was sunk in an arm chair his feet stretched out on a leather hassock. He had the thin, downcurving, bitter mouth of a morphine addict. There was sickness and death in his face. He had high blood pressure, bad kidneys, a weak heart. He was talking now about his health.

"A doctor here gave me injections of iodine to reduce the blood pressure, and the iodine has upset my whole metabolism. If I eat salt my feet swell up like that . . ." he made a gesture to indicate swelling. "And I used to be tough as nails!" he said plaintively.

He talked vaguely about going to the States for a check up at the Mayo Brothers Clinic, of moving to Costa Rica.

I nodded, waiting for him to get back to the Putumayo.

The object of my trip to Colombia was to find out all I could about a narcotic vine used by the Amazon Indians. The scientific name for this vine is *Banisteria Caapi*. There are many Indian names, since the vine is used throughout the Amazon Basin. In the Putumayo area it is called *yagé*. Other Indian names are *ayahuasca, pilde, nepi, nateema* (this last among the Jívaro of Ecuador). I had decided to start with the Putumayo area since it is readily accessible, and the Kofán Indians of the Putumayo are known to prepare a particularly potent brew of *yagé*.

Before leaving the States I had read all the material I could find on the subject. There was not much, and what there was seemed imprecise and contradictory.

The Indians call *yagé* a Soul Vine and it is used by medicine men to potentate their psychic powers. After taking *yagé* they allegedly can locate lost or stolen objects, read the thoughts of others, diagnose disease, foresee the future, and obtain knowledge of distant objects and events. The pharmacist Cardenas, who in 1923 isolated two alkaloids from the *Caapi* vine, was so impressed by the psychic properties attributed to this narcotic, that he called one of the alkaloids *Telepathine*. Telepathine is chemically identical with Harmaline, the active principle of *Perganum Harmala*, which grows in North Africa and the Mediterranean area, though there is no botanical relation between Harmala and *Banisteria Caapi*.

In a booklet called *Yagé, A Marvelous Plant*, by Jorge Barragán there are instructions for extracting the *yagé* brew for consumption, and for isolating the alkaloids. The booklet contains various anecdotes illustrating the psychic properties of *yagé*, anecdotes of the: "I took *yagé* and dreamed my great aunt had died in Río Bamba. Two days later I found out she had in fact died the night of my dream" pattern.

I have a special interest in narcotics. I have taken Peyote with Indians in Mexico, I have smoked hashish in Morocco, used cocaine, opiates, barbiturates, benzedrine, and known the horrors of drug psychosis from an overdose of hyocine. I have the subjective cellular knowledge of drugs that would enable me to compare, evaluate and classify a narcotic that I had not already experienced.

I am interested in telepathy, foresight and clairvoyance, the ESP phenomena studied by Rhine, Warcollier and others and have experimented with thought transference. So I had two reasons for interesting myself in *yagé*.

The German was talking again:

"There is a bug in the Putumayo . . . I forget what they call it, like a big grasshopper [. . .]"

## Appendix 5

## From Burroughs' March 1956 "*Yagé* Article" manuscript

### *Yagé*

Waiting for a train in Grand Central, I bought one of those he-man *True* magazines, and read an article about a lurid narcotic known as *yagé* or *ayahuasca* used by Indians of the Amazon:

"A mysterious drug known variously as *yagé, ayahuasca, pilde, nateema,* is used by the Indians of the Amazon Basin to induce a trance state in which they are said to read the thoughts of others, locate missing or stolen objects, diagnose and prescribe for diseases that have baffled the skill of modern science, and to foretell the future. One of the most remarkable powers attributed to this drug, is the ability to see and describe in accurate detail, cities and places never seen or heard of by the aborigines of these remote jungle regions. A Danish explorer tells of a Medicine Man of the Kofán tribe who, under the effects of *yagé*, described in detail the business district of Copenhagen, even writing out street signs though in a normal state he was completely illiterate."

Colonel Frijoles Barbasco de Carne of the Colombian Marines, relates the following story: "At that time I was stationed at the remote jungle outpost of Candiru, so named from a tiny, eel like fish that infests the rivers of that area. This vicious fish introduces itself into the most intimate parts of the human body, maintaining itself there by poisonous barbs while it feeds on the soft membranes.

"I had left my great aunt in the capital suffering from a serious illness. Arriving at my post, I discovered that the wireless was broken, so I would have to wait some weeks for news of my great aunt. Noting my perturbation of mind, an Indian servant urged me to take an infusion of *yagé*. I followed his suggestion, and that night had an extraordinarily vivid dream in which I saw my great aunt in a coffin surrounded by my entire family. A fortnight later I received word from the capital. My great aunt was dead, and the wake had been held the night of my dream."

Two years later I was planning a trip to the Amazon area, and I decided to check on *yagé*. A trip to the public library convinced me that such a narcotic does exist, but I could not learn much more than that. References to *yagé* were vague and contradictory. I gathered that the informants had not taken *yagé* themselves, but were merely repeating unconfirmed statements they had heard from someone else. I did learn that the scientific name for *yagé* is *Banisteria Caapi*. Since it is used throughout the Amazon Basin by various Indian tribes speaking perhaps a hundred different languages (there are 35 Indian languages in Peru alone), there are many Indian names: *yagé, ayahuasca, nepi, nateema*, this last used by the Jívaro head hunters of Peru and Ecuador.

Obviously if I was to gather any accurate information it would have to be done at first hand. I was prepared for anticlimax. A friend of mine, a botanist, went to Southern Mexico to investigate a sensational narcotic known as *ololuiqui*. Women are said to put this drug secretly in a man's food with the result that he loses all will power and becomes a helpless slave to the woman. Why the use of *ololuiqui* should be a monopoly of the female sex I don't know.

I asked my friend what he found out.

He replied: "*Ololuiqui* is a form of nutmeg." (See footnote.)*

I stopped off in Panama for yellow fever shots. Same old Panama. [. . .]

*Nutmeg is sometimes used by convicts desperate for kicks. About a tablespoon is swallowed with water. Results are somewhat similar to marijuana, but headache and nausea are usual side effects. As one nutmeg user expressed it: "Man, it's really a rough route."

---

From Bogotá I flew down to Lima, since I intended to visit the Peruvian Amazon. Lima is in a coastal desert. The city and the area immediately surrounding it is irrigated by the River Rimac. Outside the irrigated area, the landscape is dead and empty as the moon. It never rains in Lima, but during the Winter months — (their Winter is our Summer) — a heavy mist comes down from the Andes at twilight and covers the city.

You see vultures everywhere, roosting on buildings and statues in the center of town, always wheeling overhead as if they were waiting for all Lima to die.

There is a high incidence of T.B. in Lima, and bloody spit all over the streets. Lima is full of open vistas, wide streets, parks and vast, rubble strewn lots. A peculiar languor permeates the city. At all hours boys and young men loll in the parks, sleeping on the grass, or just lying there doing nothing. In the poorer quarters of the city, sanitary facilities are evidently inadequate. In any vacant lot you see people lined up along adobe walls relieving themselves. A city of great open spaces, enchanted languor, weed grown parks, vultures wheeling in a violet sky, and boys spitting blood in the street.

The Wholesale Market — Mercado Mayorista — covers several blocks. In all South American towns the market is a center of life. The Lima market is full of little bars and Chinese restaurants open twenty four hours a day. The Peruvian folk music is on the juke boxes. Boys play these tunes and dance with each other or alone. Peruvians love to dance. Fights continually break out for no apparent reason. Ramming a broken glass into your opponent's face seems to be standard practice in Peruvian bars. Everyone does it.

The national drink of Peru is Pisco, a raw cane whisky. After drinking this stuff for a week I came down with neuritis, and had to take a course of vitamin B injections. After that I switched to cognac.

Lima has an extensive Chinatown with restaurants that serve real Chinese food. There are also good Italian restaurants, and the native Creole dishes are quite tasty. Food is good and cheap. You do not feel the influence of Spain in Lima. There are, of course, Spanish colonial buildings in Lima, but the atmosphere of the city is not Spanish. Lima is pure South America, a city like no other place on earth.

After spending a week in Lima, I flew down to Pucallpa which is on the Ucayali River, a large tributary of the Amazon. Pucallpa is an end of the road town like Mocoa. In most small, South American towns they never have what you want in the shops. If the place is insufferably hot

94

there are no cold drinks. A river town will stock no fish hooks. A place infested with mosquitoes never heard of citronella. There is something intentional in this, a determination to be stupid and jerk water, a negativistic hostility, a deep self depreciation. But Pucallpa has what you want. Alert, intelligent personnel in shops and restaurants.

I stayed at the Hotel Pucallpa, and the manager was extremely helpful when I told him I was interested in *yagé*. (It is called *ayahuasca* in this area.)

My first contact was a farmer who was supposed to know all about *ayahuasca*. He turned out to be a fountain of nonsense and misinformation. Told us about a *Brujo* who took *yagé* then vomited up a full grown viper and then ate the viper again. And when the *Brujo* took *yagé* his spirits would come and shake the house.

The hotel manager then introduced me to the local "Doctor," a man named Saboya — (A Doctor only works cures whereas a *Brujo* deals in both cures and curses)—Saboya was an unassuming young man. He readily agreed to prepare *yagé* for me.

I met the Doctor in his hut on the outskirts of town. There were six Indians there, two of them women — (evidently the taboo on women does not apply here) — and we went out and sat under the trees. The Doctor poured a cup of *yagé* mixture out of a beer bottle into a cup and whistled over it the *Yagé pintar* song I remembered from Colombia. Then he handed me the cup. Every time he filled the cup he whistled over it before passing it out to drink. Nobody talked or made any noise.

I experienced at first a feeling of calm and serenity like I could sit there all night. I glimpsed a new state of being. I must give up the attempt to explain, to seek any answer in terms of cause and effect and prediction, leave behind the entire structure of pragmatic, result seeking, use seeking, question asking Western thought. I must change my whole method of conceiving fact.

A blue substance seemed to invade my body. I saw an archaic, grinning face like a South Pacific mask. The face was blue-purple splotched with gold. My jaws clamped tight and convulsive tremors started in my arms and legs. An overdose again. I took five nembutals and three grains of para-codeine, and the tremors subsided. (See Footnote) One of the women was feeling nauseated. The Doctor put his mouth against hers and went through a pantomime of sucking something out of her body. Then he turned aside and pretended to vomit.

I felt cold and mosquitoes were biting me and I wanted to go to bed. At once the Doctor said: "Mister wants to go." It was completely dark. He could not see me, and I had made no movement.

After that night I bought bottles of prepared solution from the Doctor and took it a number of times. Considerable tolerance is acquired. After the second dose I experienced no nausea or other ill effects. This is the most powerful drug I have ever experienced. That is it produces the most complete derangement of the senses. You see everything from an halluci-nated viewpoint. *Yagé* is not like anything else. This is not the electric euphoria of coke which activates channels of pure pleasure in the brain, the sexless, timeless, negative pleasure of opium. It is closer to hashish than to any other drug. There are also similarities between Peyote and *yagé*. But

*Footnote:* Any strong sedative is the antidote for an overdose of *yagé*. It is advisable to provide oneself with a sedative before experimenting with *yagé*. A few months before my arrival, a man died from an overdose near Mocoa.

while hashish intensifies all sensual impressions, *yagé* distorts or shuts out ordinary sensations, transporting you to another level of experience.

*Notes from Yagé State:* The room takes on a Near Eastern aspect with blue walls and red tasseled lamps. I feel myself turning into a Negro, the black color silently invading my flesh. My legs take on a well rounded, Polynesian substance. Everything stirs with a writhing, furtive life. The room is Near Eastern and South Pacific and in some familiar but unde-fined place. I notice in lighter intoxication the effect is Near Eastern, in deeper intoxication South Pacific — (Suggestion of phylogenetic mem-ory. Migration from Near East to South America to South Pacific.) — There is a feeling of space time travel that seems to shake the room. It occurs to me that preliminary *yagé* nausea is motion sickness of transport to *yagé* state.

The Doctor has showed me his method of preparing *yagé* — (Usually a trade secret) — He mashes pieces of the fresh cut vine and boils two hours with the leaves of another plant tentatively identified by a Peruvian botanist as *Palicourea Species Rubiaceae*. The effect of *yagé* prepared in this manner is qualitatively different from cold water infusion of *yagé* alone, or *yagé* cooked alone. The other leaf is essential to realize the full effect of the drug. Whether it is itself active, or merely serves as a catalyzing agent, I do not know. This matter needs the attention of a chemist.

I have experimented with tinctures, dried preparations, and none of them have any effect. Dried vines are completely inactive. Only the fresh cut vine prepared in the manner described is effective.

Went back to Lima by car. I was hung up two days in Huánuco. [. . .]

---

## Appendix Summary

*Banisteria Caapi* is a fast growing vine that reaches a length of sixty feet and a diameter of three inches. The active principle is apparently found throughout the wood of the fresh cut vine, but the inner bark is considered most active, and the wood core often thrown away. The leaves are never used. It takes a considerable quantity of vine to make enough extract to feel the full effect of the drug. About five pieces of vine each eight inches long are needed for one person. (The vine is usually one and one half to two inches in diameter.) — The vine is crushed and boiled for two or more hours with the leaves of a bush identified as *Palicourea Sp. Rubiaceae*. About a double handful of leaves per person is put on top of the crushed *Banisteria* vine, water added, and the mixture boiled without stirring.

*Yagé* or *ayahuasca*, the most commonly used Indian names for *Banisteria Caapi*, is a hallucinating narcotic that produces a profound derangement of the senses. In overdose it is a convulsant poison for which the antidote is a barbiturate or other strong, anti-convulsant sedative. Anyone taking *yagé* for the first time should have a sedative ready to take in the event of an overdose.

The hallucinating properties of *yagé* have led to its use by medicine men to potentate their powers. They also use it as a sort of cure-all in the treatment of various illnesses. *Yagé* lowers the body temperature, and consequently is of some use in the treatment of fever. It is also a powerful anthelmintic, indicated for conditions of stomach or intestinal worms. *Yagé* induces a state of conscious anesthesia, and is used in rites where the initiates must undergo a painful ordeal like whipping with knotted vines, or the stings of ants.

Whether the drug actually influences ESP, I was not able to discover since I had no one with me to conduct experiments in thought transference. Certainly ESP experiments with *yagé* should be carried out.

So far as I could discover only the fresh cut vine is active. I found no way to dry, extract, or preserve the active principle. No tinctures proved active. The dried vine is completely inert. The pharmacology of *yagé* requires laboratory research. Since the crude extract is such a powerful, hallucinating narcotic, probably even more spectacular results could be obtained with stronger, synthetic variations. Certainly the matter warrants further research.

I did not observe any ill effects that could be attributed to the use of *yagé*. The medicine men who use it continually in line of duty seem to enjoy normal health and longevity. Tolerance is soon acquired so that one can drink the extract without nausea or other ill effects.

*Yagé* is a unique narcotic. The experience of *yagé* is in some respects similar to hashish. In both instances there is a shift of viewpoint, an extension of experience beyond ordinary consciousness. *Yagé* produces a deeper derangement of the senses, more tendency to hallucination. The whole *yagé* experience is less under control, further out. This loss of control can be extremely terrifying until you learn not to fight against it.

I have observed in using both *yagé* and Peyote a strange, vegetable consciousness, an identification with the plant. In Peyote intoxication everything looks like a Peyote plant. It is easy to understand how the Indians came to believe there is a spirit in these plants.

There is a wide range of attitude in regard to *yagé*. Many users seem to regard it simply as another intoxicant like liquor. They use it, quite frankly, for kicks. In other groups it has ritual use and significance. Among the Jívaro young men take *yagé* — *nateema* they call it — to contact the spirits of their ancestors and get a briefing for their future life. It is used in initiations to anesthetize the initiates for painful ordeals. All medicine men use it in their practice to foretell the future, locate lost or stolen objects, name the perpetrator of a crime, to diagnose and treat illness.

The bibliography on *yagé* is sketchy, much of it inaccurate repetition of unconfirmed statements. A booklet entitled *Notes on the Marvelous Plant Yagé* by Jorge Barragán, put out in Popayán, Colombia, 1928, contains much useful information. The alkaloid of *yagé* was isolated in 1923 by Fisher Cardenas. He called the alkaloid *Telepathine*. It is also known as Banisterine or Yageina. Rumf showed that Telepathine is chemically identical with Harmine, the alkaloid of *Perganum Harmala*.

There are references to *yagé* in the following works:

*Enumeración botánica* [*de las principales plantas*] [1911] by Luis Cordero
*Vegetación del Ecuador* [1937] by [Diels] Ludwig
*Notes of a Botanist* [*on the Amazon and Andes*] [1908] by Richard Spruce
*Plant Alkaloids* [1913] by [Thomas Anderson] Henry
*Viaje por el Caqueta y Putumayo* [1924?] by Darío Rozo [Martínez]

The most complete collection of material on *yagé* is to be found in the Botanical Museum of Harvard University.

# Appendix 6

## From Ginsberg's June 1960 South American Journal

June 6, 1960

Ayahuasca —
Moonlit nite
entered bamboo roof shelter
lay on ground on robe
— entered the Great Being
        again
— we are all one Great Being
        whose presence is familiar
— To be It, need to be
        also the mosquito
            that bites me
— I am also a mosquito
        on the Great Being

———————————————

June 8 Ayahuasca in Pucallpa — yesterday

First saw a Spectrum of different designs colored somewhat like
Chama (Shipibo) pottery & blankets I'd seen all day — then the different

beads of color took on organic forms—flies, bees, golden bugs, Serpents, many serpents, a myriad of miniature serpents making a great sheath or star of visual fabric in front of a great intelligent hole, an empty black space like the entrance to the great personal Nose of God — where I stared in—somewhat like the vision of Krishna in Bhagavad-Gita—and this existed in front of me, at once a little scary, but very little, and mostly very pleasant & personal, intimate, old tune familiar—the mind's entrance into god similar in sentiment to the cock's entrance into cunt—this great creature being bisexual and the lover of all in an extremely secret personal way — he tends the bees and the frogs as well as me.

The mosquitoes interrupted my contemplation—Kept buzzing and at times settling down on my flesh to bite—finally I came to point of extension of my body throughout universe, that I began to accept the noise as part of the music—locusts, frogs, dogbarks—of the night all crying aloud in communication of the Name of the Great Being of which they were a part—and without moving I allowed several to bite me—still disturbed—tho I created a voice in my soul which said, from Above—"You have to be a mosquito too, Allen"—said very dearly. This the condition of entrance complete into the Great Being—Thought of Kerouac on car roof in night across Mexico Border—allowing mosquitoes to seep into his body, giving himself up to the Universal activity of the night. What transcendency, then, did he know at that moment? Surely more than pure will power—perhaps he actually gave up his Self for that Great Mess of Creation.

The voice and the Great Being is that of the Father's Father's Father, a Father way back, lover to each creature — very busy supplying each creature with his proper inevitable Honey & Death. So, much like the Great Queen maggot of the African movie saw in N.Y. last year.

Also, that I am a mosquito-type creature in relation to the Divine, that I suck off the divine, who is in long run my one deepest lover —

Realization (over again) that the world is so illusory that what can be communicated, said, writ, in terms of human consciousness bears no relation to the Great Being who is complete in Itself and so perfect that no complaint need be made — it's all one mess which eats itself — to separate from the process of Death & attempt to preserve the Good of Individual beings is vain, because the Deepest part of each is the Great Deathless Love Beast whose mosquitoes and Bacteria have to eat too — each one has his murderous needs in creation, God can't favor us over the mosquitoes without murdering & starving mosquitoes — So he lets us fight it out outside himself in chaos of Illusion, always retaining the Final Great Black Hole of Love to which we can return after death of Individuality when we have been defeated or become tired of being separate individuals in creation — normal consciousness of the merely human self.

Had lain out for long time several hours in bamboo cookshelter outside Maestro's house (Flaviano?) & Ramon had got up, & told me to wrap myself in his mantle to protect me from mosquitoes. A very kind gesture, I felt he realized I too had climbed up thru the Nose of God into Being the Same as Ramon — that we were all one, and this was a kindly gesture (wrought from afar by god) to protect me in my as yet delicate individuality — later I went in the house, where they were (4 of them having drunk), sensing a great feeling of communal fraternity & sharing of realization of Infinite Intimacy — one old fellow on a bench, an albanil, moved over & motioned me welcome to join him next to him to sit down. I saw they in Pucallpa had their own secret transcendental nosey society, underneath very humane, in huts. And the Indians, Chamas, outside too.

The familiar creepy sexy nosey personal intimate old-known special re-realization of the Joke sweetness of Illusion fading into the Great Black Asshole of one-Mind one-Love cat-faced snake-faced dog-faced man-faced Mandalic Universal Newspaper Busybody Gossip God. All mine, all everybody's, all everything's. And what else could He be but He Himself?

———————

The Curandero-Maestro's ceremony — he being ill — was to dip an enamel cup into a tin pot full of green-brown liquor, hold it in front of mouth, smoking cigarette, & whistle a sad tune thru the smoke, following up with humming extension of same tune into the tomb of the cup thru the smoke, then pass it on to me to light a cigarette, blow smoke into the surface of the beer, and drink up.

"If the Slayer thinks he is Slain . . ." How did the Great Being communicate with Emerson & the Transcendentalists? What states of consciousness & feeling did Emerson know?

———————

Thus on the human level the method of approach soul to soul on the most intimate level of mutual concern begins to approximate the relation of Soul to God — thus humans as lovers & caretakers & fathers make the Eternal Scene. This intimacy constantly violated by hard hearted madness & politics & business & war.

Thus the saint is the delicate-handed intimate of all — St. Francis and the Birds — recognizing Brotherhood. No morals but Love.

———————

There's no need to communicate the News of God. Those who seek, find. Those who need something else get something else — get trapped in the separate universe of their own making — but are disintegrated and rejoined to the Great Being, surprised, at one time or another, perhaps after Death — which is Death only of separate consciousness. All's taken care of in Perfection.

———

The Police in Pucallpa are beginning to persecute the Ayahuasca drinkers and Curanderos — pressure from local Bureaucracy — Doctors who have no experience of the Mystery of the Beer. A Materialistic consciousness is attempting to preserve itself from Dissolution by restriction & persecution of Experience of the Transcendental. One day perhaps the Earth will be dominated by the Illusion of Separate consciousness, the Bureaucrats having triumphed in seizing control of all roads of communication with the Divine, & restricting traffic. But Sleep & Death cannot evade the Great Dream of Being, and the victory of the Bureaucrats of Illusion is only an Illusion of their separate world of consciousness. The suffering caused is only temporary, and makes no difference in the Last Judgment of the Soul when it returns to itself, realizing that the Great Inner Universe always exists in the same person and is Eternal despite the transient vanities of the busybodies of Time.

I am only a busybody meddling in human affairs vainly trying to assert the Supremacy of the Soul — which can take care of itself without me & my egoistic assumption of the Divine, my presumption that the Eternal needs my assistance to exist & preserve itself in the world. All my worry's as much of a Joke as the equal worry of the police. We are all trapped in the Divine Honey, like flies, struggling in different ways to accommodate ourselves.

———————

The struggle & Pain of Death is only the Soul being forced to recognize its Final nature & leave the Separate Individual Self.

———————

Poverty, hunger, suffering also separate the soul from the body, the temporary body, and serve as exercises of the Divine. Tho it is painful — somebody has to suffer, the man or his ox.

———————

The reward annihilates the Struggle. God is Perfect.

———————————————

June 8? — 9? Ayahuasca Session —

Lay back an hour, waiting for something to happen, nothing did, I just went right on thinking, what was I looking for, anyway, Something Real about the Universe? And slowly crept up on me that I was in a real Universe — and had been for many years now in this body — and that this body was changing, was isolated, but this isolation in the body of Allen Ginsberg which was my life up to now, would inevitably change — began to sense a strange Presence in the hut — a Blind Being — or a being I am blind to habitually — like a science fiction Radiotelepathy Beast from another Universe — but from this series of universes in which I do temporarily exist—So temporarily that the presence of the Beast was a warning of the Future—my body began to shake slightly—I realized protecting it from mosquitoes & sickness was only temporary remedy & unconsciousness of The Final Proposition of To Be or Not to Be, the Death which will come to me one day soon, soon enough for me to think of it as real as this life — and suddenly I felt nausea with life itself, my body quaking with fear & self disgust at so temporary a Being doomed—I felt doomed to Futurity, doomed in Futurity, even if I escape it by poetry queer vanity sex assfucking riding around the world being Loverboy of Boys Allen all my life—sooner or later his lonely farce to be extinguished all this illusion dropped & the skull of Ultimate Reality with its Death rear its head — (O dear Beard in Frisco Angel who taught me, high, oldage sickness & Death, Hube the Cube, Seraph, with strange shoulder message of "Blessed Blessed oblivion.") — I staggered out on the porch and into the garden to vomit, began regurgitating up my sense of Permanence & Security, began vomiting up life—all around the noise of vomit, of the universe vomiting up parts of itself — the snake that eats itself vomiting itself back forth into Being—I was a vomiting snake, that is I vomited with eyes closed and sensed myself a Serpent of Being, or Serpent of Illusion, a serpent of Isolation, the Serpent of Allen, covered with Aureole of spiky snakeheads miniatured radiant & many colored around my hands & throat — my throat bulging like the Beast of Creation, like the Beast of Death—to vomit forth my physical misery to Be — I heaved it out four or five times & remained standing in a trance horrified at my Serpent Self — meanwhile the Curandero was continually crooning to the 30 people dreaming entranced in the Universe all connected telepathically to this one Being who expressed one of his aspects thru the tender plaintive almost motherly crooning—"Nu nu nu, nu nu, nu, nu nu nu"—I stood in the full moonlight with eyes closed feeling my skull vomiting forth in life knowing the vomit was a little death, only a sign of the frailty of this body, a Sign of What is to Come to the Body—the Great Death which'll envelop it—and communicate itself to the Body, in Time, we can't Escape Trapped, I am trapped in being myself—for tho I cherish myself now & protect me from mosquitoes—take tablets to avoid vomit—one day Death will vomit me out of this body—returning to my pallet after a kind word from Seraph Ramon, who asked me how I was and if I were "mareado" (drunk enough yet)? —I saw a man who was sitting leaning against a post with knees drawn up to his breasts—covered with cloth against the mosquitoes—like a mummy in Chancay Necropolis' 1000 year old sands—million year old sands—I saw his white shrouded face, as if in X ray the hallucination for a moment of seeing thru to the Living Bone that he is as all men as I—going to die—and lay down (worried that I might hex him by dwelling on his skull, staring at it too long). I bethought me of my own skull to come & entered such a state of Mortal Misery as I had not ever encountered in conscious life—the realization that we are set here to live and Die, and all man set here together in different bodies in a web of realization of the same fate—and I gave myself more up to this mystery—until my head shook back and forth in resignation and defeat, and I gave my fate over back to God who made it—Questioned whether I was yet prepared to Die—The God seemingly discarnate but incarnate in the community of Beings all experiencing the same realization of their Dying

Bodies in Strange & Unknown spacetime fate — the gentle crooning continuing — I wanted to know if there were some Answer, some way out of Fate, some entrance to Perfection which would include both Death & Life, both Allen & Allen's dry indifferent skull — no answer — but saw Christ lifted on the Cross of Death, suffering — I felt Christ — we are all Christ — our Souls are all preparing to be Crucified — for real — "Let this cup pass from me?" but no it will not pass — and I lay there with arms extended for a moment, sighing giving myself up to my defeat, my ignorance of what is and what's to be & Who I am & the purpose of the game of being poet playing with great Words when the Divine Fire is At Hand, so real, to Be, and to come, and to Die — and the sensation of a presence beyond it all — the void has a billion entrances, a billion deaths — and births — that Billion doored Not Paradise Not Known yet by me only myriad different glimpses of Something afar — now Near me — all Creation alive — all beings perhaps the only part we can know — That God lives in us, not otherwise — that *we*, *here*, are it, the great Presence, *we* are the great Presence of the Universe, our consciousness is the consciousness of the Last Thing — that God himself knows no more than we or I why he was born or where he is going, it is all in us to live or die, to change the Universe or leave it, to be or not to be — and I lay back with my near deadlike body & skull on the mantle and accepted the question there & then — to Escape Being *Now*! And avoided the question — a sudden fear realization that if I chose then to die I might be found by others a corpse in the morn, and news of Allen's death in Drugs reach New York — and scare Peter & grieve Louis — who knows I am sick of Life — but who still thinks I will choose to live — or who still hopes I will come into contact with life again, with women & love creation — I got scared thinking then that I had the power to die then & there — tho I didn't have the power, I was scared of *that* much power, I shrank back into prayer "In thy Will is my peace" and said "I don't want to die" knowing that if I don't want to die now, when will I ever and yet die I soon must someday & the Great Choice will again confront me — "To reach that Door" — (Hardy) — I began dreaming of all the living whom I knew — Peter, afar, who looks on me for Help, for Love, for Salvation, for Spiritual Knowledge — and I know nothing — God perhaps knows nothing, it is all up to us, he gives the life to us, his life to us, as He, mysterious, without known origin and with unknown end — we are given the Woes of God, we are the God, in existence in the Universe — looking out with open eye at the bright nite sky — clouds a veil of Bethlehem over the Stars of other Sister or Brother Friend worlds of this same ancient sad familiar mystery Universe —

# Notes

## Key to Abbreviations:

YAGE ms. = Burroughs' June 1953 manuscript of what became "In Search of Yage" (Ginsberg Collection, Stanford University).

YA = Burroughs' 1956 manuscript of his "*Yagé* Article": first draft, January 1956; second draft, March 1956 (Burroughs Collection, Columbia University).

GC, CU = Ginsberg Collection, Columbia University

BC, CU = Burroughs Collection, Columbia University

Unless stated, all letters cited are in *The Letters of William S. Burroughs, 1945–1959* (New York: Viking, 1993).

3   "I stopped off here": before an insert revised the opening lines, the YAGE ms. began; **"When I went to Colombia to score for Yage I was walking into strange territory cold. ~~I stopped off in Panama for typhoid and yellow fever shots.~~"** (Note that Burroughs always misspelled the place name as "Columbia"; corrected in all ms. quotations.)

3   "back to Mexico": the YAGE ms. has an extra deleted line; **"We separated hating each other like old Joe and the Black Bastard."** (See *Junky*, where Joe [Tesorero] appears as Old Ike.)

3   "I checked into the hospital" to "hernia case": these lines do not appear on the YAGE ms., which had; **"Spent a nightmarish four days in the hospital half sick with a sore ass and only 4 skimpy shots of M. There was a Panamanian . . ."** In the ms. it is friends **"and relatives"** who stay half the night **"chattering like monkeys"**.

4   "After checking out" to "two ounces of paregoric": these lines do not appear on the YAGE ms.

4   "I remembered a Prohibition era road house": in an aside on the YAGE ms., Burroughs commented; **"A little drunk and sentimental I committed the following atrocity where I describe the Blue Goose. In all seriousness too. Get a load of this: 'I remembered [. . .] Mid West Summer.' Oh My God. How sloppy can you get? 'And the warm Spring wind and Billy Bradshinkel's cock' — This last was, of course, not part of original lapse into typical young U.S. novelist style. But satirical comment on same."**

5   "The Panamanians are about the crummiest people in the Hemisphere": this line appears in Burroughs' letter to Ginsberg of January 19, 1953 (GC, CU).

5   "standing there in the warm spring wind": immediately before these words the YAGE ms. has the deleted phrase **"and puppy sweat on his face"** and, immediately after, the unused phrase **"with frogs croaking all around us"**. In the following paragraph, after "his smooth cheek against mine," the YAGE ms. has another unused phrase: **"and the faint smell of vomit"**.

7   "Another routine": the YAGE ms. has; **"Idea for a story."**

8   "Sunday lunch in Cincinnati!": the YAGE ms. has **"St Louis!"**

8   "Bogota is on a high plain": the YAGE ms. has a different opening; **"I flew down to Bogota which is on a high plain surrounded by mountains. I drove in from the airport in a cold windy twilight."**

9   "He suggested the Putumayo": this sentence does not appear on the YAGE ms.

10  "Made in Spain": after this line, the text in *Kulchur* continued; **"There is a civil war in Columbia [sic] between the Liberals and the Conservatives. The Liberal forces occupy Meta and make guerilla raids into the adjacent states of Tolima and Caqueta and Santandor."** The YAGE ms. has a slightly different version, including a significant extra line that runs on from "Made in Spain": **"especially the Franco stooge Laureane Gomes Dictator of the so called Republic of Colombia."** This line does not appear on the tms. of this letter which was probably part of the December 1953 ms. (BC, CU). Burroughs was certainly referring to this tms. when he indicated cutting the "last three lines after 'dead weight of Spain sombre and oppressive'" in the "Corrections" listed in his letter of January 9, 1955 (BC, CU). On the copy of the text in *Kulchur* used to make the first edition in 1963, the last four sentences (from "Everything offi-

cial" to "Santandor") are struck through (City Lights Editorial Files, Berkeley).

10 "I had a gun in my luggage": on the YAGE ms. this line begins with the phrase, **"I was a bit nervous because"**.

10 "Palace Guard": this phrase is an autograph insert on the YAGE ms., which originally identified the Policia Nacional as **"the S.S. of the Conservative Party"**. In Burroughs' letter of April 22, 1953, where the material in this whole paragraph also appears, the PN are described as the "back-bone" of the CP.

11 "If there is anything to say": before this sentence, the YAGE ms. has another line; **"Usually in a civil war there is a lot to say on both sides."** At this point YA (January 1956 ms.) has an extra line: **"The decaying corpse of the Spanish colonial Empire. They build nothing, create nothing. They only block and repress."**

11 "ugly looking shits": the YAGE ms. continues at this point, running on; **"maintaining themselves by force. A Liberal Swede I met in Cali said 'It makes me sick when I see what the Conservatives have done in this country. But they can't stop progress with all their black and gray bastards — reference to the priests and the gray uniformed Policia Nacional — Every intelligent decent person is a Liberal.' At the time I discounted this but every intelligent decent person I met in Colombia was a Liberal."** This last line appears near-verbatim in Burroughs' letter of April 22, 1953.

11 "In a hot dusty" to " innocence": these lines do not appear on the YAGE ms.

11 "on to Cali next day with the autoferro": the YAGE ms. continues, in lines struck through; **"This is far and away most comfortable way to travel in Colombia except of course flying."**

12 "financial aid": the YAGE ms. continues; **"They don't understand these people back home."**

12 "It does not occur to them that": before these lines were revised and expanded some time after June 1953, the YAGE ms. originally continued; **"the decline of white prestige is world wide and has little connection with the activities of Point Four."**

12 "no intention of buying me a drink": the YAGE ms. continues, in a line struck through; **"but hoped I would buy him one. Stalemate."**

13 "there you will find the Church": the YAGE ms. continues; **" — you will**

find a God damned priest in it up to his withered balls — (cross out
if see fit)".

14  "I wonder what his sex life could be": the YAGE ms. continues; **"Probably
sticks a crucifix up his ass — C.O.I.S.F. cross out if see fit — "**

14  "It seemed like every second person": YA has a different version; **"I walked
around in a cold, wet twilight through the streets of Pasto. This is a
high mountain town, cold, dirty and depressing. I passed dwarfs,
hunchbacks, people with boneless flippers for hands, with hair lips
[sic] and horrible skin diseases. They looked like the end result of
atomic radiation. No one smiled, no one spoke. People walked by in
silence, their faces wrapped in scarves against the night air."**

14  "I went into a cantina": the YAGE ms. has only; **"I went in a cantina and
played the juke box oriental music with the deep sadness of the high
mountains."** The rest of this paragraph was an addition revised in January
1955.

15-16  "I had an introduction" to "I'm stuck": these paragraphs were given as
"notes for insertion" to the YAGE ms. in Burroughs' letter to Ginsberg of June
8, 1953 (GC, CU). Another version of this material, now in epistolary form,
is found together with the YA ms. (January 1956), where it was reworked into
a new narrative frame (see Appendix 4).

16  "Will leave here" to "responsibility": this paragraph was not part of the insert
given in Burroughs' letter of June 8, 1953 (see above), but does appear in the version found with the YA ms. and derives probably from the December 1953 ms.

16  "On my way back" to "chronologically": none of this paragraph is in the
YAGE ms., but a version of some lines appears in Burroughs' letter of March
1, 1953.

17  "Not even citronella": the YAGE ms. has a line in between dashes here; **"The
more mosquitoes a place has the harder it is to buy citronella — "**

17  "for all eternity": the YAGE ms. continues; **" — None of this conveys the
horror of Mocoa. Something is always between me and the fact
which I feel but can't communicate.** ~~What I need is a 'flash'. Anybody
who 'flashed' Mocoa would drop dead on the spot. One thing I
know.~~ **The situation calls for wholesale massacre. Young boys doing
strip teases with the intestines of the Policia Nacional and the entire
population high on Yage. Then Mocoa must be raised [sic] to the
ground and ploughed under and returned to the jungle — It is an**

abomination in the sight of the living." (Note that Burroughs always misspelled the place name as "Macoa"; corrected in all ms. quotations.)

19   "Why not?": YA continues; **"Game is scarce. We saw a few parrots and small monkeys, one two-toed sloth. The Indian told me the sloth is considered excellent food. There are few dangerous animals in the South American jungle. Jaguars rarely attack human beings. There are snakes, of course, and I never went into the jungle without anti-venom and a syringe. There is considerable doubt as to whether the old routine of slashing the fang holes with a razor blade and applying potassium permanganate does any good. The only really effective remedy is anti-venom, the sooner applied the better."**

19   "could have walked twice that far": YA continues; **"A friend of mine, a botanist who works for Point Four, told me that the U.S. Army was interested in *yoka* at one time. A substance that prevents hunger and fatigue for six to eight hours would have obvious military applications. So my friend collected some specimens and sent them back to the U.S. Analysis showed that *yoka* contains caffeine and tannin in very large quantities. A cup of *yoka* infusion contains about the quantity of caffeine found in twenty cups of coffee."**

19   "pieces they consider non-essential": the YAGE ms. continues with a line in parentheses struck through; **"(They think the gringos don't know how to make motors)."**

19   "God knows why": this phrase was struck through in type on the YAGE ms. but retained for all editions, whereas a further line on the ms. was not used; **"Typical hick thinking."** YA had an alternative final line: **"The stupid are unfathomable."**

19   "Next day the governor": parts of this paragraph overlap Burroughs' letter of March 1, 1953. YA gives more detail about what it refers to as **"the Corregidor"; "This is a civilian official, a combination mayor and police commissioner."**

20   "a beat look in his eyes": the YAGE ms. (and YA) has **"beaten"** rather than "beat".

20   "vitamin B tablets": the YAGE ms. continues with another line, crossed out; **"It was poltergeistish."**

21   "sign language": the YAGE ms. continues with another line, crossed out; **"At least this kid had no pretensions to a mastery of English."**

21 "and off my ass": the YAGE ms. continues with another line; **"No doubt about the come on now."**

21 "when he told me" to "steal my skivvies": the line occurs in Burroughs' letter to Ginsberg of April 30, 1953 (GC, CU).

22 "sepulchral telegrams" to "returned to Mocoa": these lines occur in Burroughs' letter of March 1, 1953, although this has "Florida" not "Ohio" (YA has "Missouri").

22 "for three days": the YAGE ms. continues; **"I was out of bed in four days and ready to travel. I went back to Bogota and had my papers corrected."**

22-23 "I will go to Bogota" to "gun point?": these lines do not appear on the YAGE ms; the lines from "Travel in Colombia" to "police" occur in Burroughs' letter of March 1, 1953.

23 "March 3": none of the material in this letter appears in the YAGE ms; the lines from "I have attached" to "Cocoa Commission" occur in Burroughs' letter of March 5, 1953.

24 "Back in Bogota" to "Flashback: Retraced": this material, which occurs in Burroughs' letter of April 12, 1953, does not appear in the YAGE ms.

24 "This trip I was treated" to "coming of Christ": this material, which derives from Burroughs' letter of April 12, 1953, does not appear in the YAGE ms.

25 "And the governor thinks" to "believe it": this material derives from the Mocoa "notes" section in Burroughs' letter of Early July 1953.

25 "they couldn't believe it": YA (January 1956 ms. used here) continues;

I paid a formal call on the governor and asked him about *yagé*. I will relate what he said as accurately as I can remember because he managed to include in his account all the myths and beliefs about *yagé* that are current in the Amazon region. I have heard exactly the same story in Peru and Ecuador. Checking closer it usually turns out the informant has never taken *yagé* himself.

The Governor: "After drinking *yagé* you see, at first, horrible visions, snakes and tigers . . . Sometimes the Indians think they have turned into animals and crawl around howling and imitating the animal they think they have turned into. This first state of fear and frenzy passes away and you lie back in a telepathic state. You can communicate with the Indians without knowing a word of their language. You see beautiful visions of cities and parks."

The Governor had several typical anecdotes illustrating the psychic properties of this drug: like the *Brujo* took *yagé* and told somebody what was happening to his great aunt in Bogotá — which was later confirmed, of course — or he located some missing object.

Finally he recommended that I visit a German who had a *finca* near Mocoa. "There is an old *Brujo* who lives out near his *finca* who knows how to prepare *yagé*. If you were introduced by the German he would certainly prepare it for you to take."

I visited the German the following day. He was married to an Indian woman and had been living there fifteen years.

27  "All I want is out of here": after this, YA has an extra line; **"I had no clear idea as to where I was or what was happening to me."**

27  "croaking of frogs": after this, YA has an extra line; **"And underlying this silliness was the unmistakable feel of mortal danger."**

27  "as if it was someone else": *Big Table* and all previous editions have "as if I was someone else," but all three available mss. (YAGE and both YA drafts) confirm "it" not "I".

28  "the Putumayo Kofan method": YA (besides identifying that the assistant comes from the **"Vaupés region of Colombia near the Venezuelan frontier"**) continues (March 1956 ms.); **"In the Vaupés, *yagé* is used in a puberty rite known as the Devil Dance. The boys who are being initiated into manhood are first drugged with *yagé*, then they must undergo a severe beating with knotted vines. Schindler's assistant showed me the scars on his back. *Yagé* causes anesthesia in a waking state so the initiates do not feel much pain."**

28  "In Putumayo the Indians cut" to "liquid": these lines rewrote the version on the YAGE ms; **"The Putumayo method is: pound about four pounds of the whole vine to a pulp and boil the pulp all day barely covered with water down to two ounces of liquid. This is recipe for one person."**

28  "The Brujo of Mocoa told me": in YA (March 1956 ms.) it is the Brujo's assistant who relates the "poisonous routine" (**"that is common among 'primitive' people throughout the world"**); **"And the *yagé* has no power unless the *Brujo* performs the appropriate ceremonies. He said all this as if repeating a lesson he had learned, and I wondered if he really believed it. There are, of course, various levels of belief. Probably he hesitated to question the whole framework of which this belief was a**

part. It would not occur to him to put the matter to the test of experiment." YA (January 1956 ms.) has a further line: **"Knowledge for the sake of knowledge has no meaning for an Indian."**

28  "chance to test": original phrasing on the YAGE ms. is not "test" but **"explode the woman pollution myth"**.

29  "In this dosage": before this line, YA (March 1956 ms. used here) has the sentence; **"I experienced the characteristic blue flashes I had noted in my first contact with *yagé*, not a flash exactly, but a point of blue light moving so rapidly across the field of vision that it appears as a blue line or streak."**

29  "A coolness": this is followed on the YAGE ms. by an unused phrase; **"progressing to deep freeze"**.

29  "expedition to the nearest finca": this line replaced the longer version, deleted on the YAGE ms; **"Typical scene on the way back from one of these expeditions to the nearest finca. The Colombians giving orders to their assistant to cut down a tree they wanted a specimen of vine growing on the tree. The British watched this activity in cool silence. One of them said to me out of the corner of his mouth. 'So long as they can collect any old weed they don't give a ruddy fuck.'"**

29  "There was supposed to be plane service out of Puerto Espina": before this line the YAGE ms. has; **"Schultes [sic] got disgusted with the situation and went on down to Puerto Leguizamo to take a plane back to Bogota."** After it, the ms. continues: **"The airline had an agent there but he did not know when or if the plane would come and had no way to find out since his radio was broken. Every day I asked him about the plane and he said he thought the plane would sure be there in a week or so."** (Note that Burroughs always misspelled the place name as "Puerto Leguisomo"; corrected in all ms. quotations.)

29-30  "so there we sit" to "the Commandante is Latah": this material derives from a distinct ms. page, gathered together with the YAGE ms. but written on a different typewriter at a later date.

30  "start and die all night": the YAGE ms. continues; **"knowing you will likely be stuck there another day"**.

30-31  "(Latah is" to "same bullshit": these lines do not appear on the YAGE ms.

31  "the use of a narcotic": among minor unused material, the YAGE ms. has an extra line here; **"'And lay off those platanos' I added silently."**

118

**32** "The Colombians run" to "the conference": these lines derive from Burroughs' letter of April 12, 1953.

**32** "Puerto Leguizamo is named" to "*something*": these lines do not appear on the YAGE ms.

**32** "Peruvian War of 1940": YA has an extra line; **"(When Colombians talk about 'the War' this is generally the one referred to)."** Note that I have preferred the phrasing "of 1940" from *Big Table* (and YA), where previous editions had "in 1940"—although in fact neither is historically correct, since the Colombian-Peruvian "war" took place in July 1941.

**32** "Inquiring in the environs": for the YAGE ms. from this point until its end, see Appendix 1.

**33** "No money waiting" to "visiting scientist": these lines occur in Burroughs' letter of April 22, 1953, although the version on the YAGE ms. differs slightly here.

**33** "Extracting Yage alkaloids": YA (January 1956 ms.) has a different version; **"I extracted the alkaloids from some *yagé* vines I had brought back with me according to directions provided in a booklet entitled *Yagé* by Gorge Barragán. A comparatively simple process. My experiments with extracted *yagé* were not conclusive. I never obtained from it the same effects as are produced by the crude extract. In fact the only result I obtained from the alkaloid was drowsiness. I can only conclude that I made some error in the process of extraction, since I am not a chemist and have little experience in laboratory techniques."**

**33-34** "Every night" to "empty house": these lines are almost all given as "notes for insertion" in Burroughs' letter of June 8, 1953 (GC, CU). After "empty house," YA continues (longer, March 1956 version): **"Unlike Europe or Asia, South America has no basic economic problems. It is an under-populated country with more room and more land than the present inhabitants can use. Civil war is understandable in a poor, crowded country like Spain where there isn't enough to go around. But why in Colombia?"**

**34** "This finds me" to "exiled from Rome": lines derive from Burroughs' letter of May 5, 1953.

**35** "Small country" to "stage": line derives from Burroughs' letter of June 8, 1953 (GC, CU), which continues; **"I am reminded of the cartoon. The psychiatrist saying to patient: 'Don't worry about it, Mr. Crumb. You *should* have an inferiority complex.'"**

**35** "Ecuadorian Miscellanea" to "balls": lines derive from the "Ecuadorian miscellanea" in Burroughs' letter of June 6, 1953.

**35** "The inevitable Turk" to "late": lines derive from the Esmeraldas notes in Burroughs' letter of Early July 1953.

**35** "On the boat" to "Auca boy": lines derive from Burroughs' letter to Ginsberg of April 30, 1953 (GC, CU).

**35** "Arriving in Manta" to "inspector": lines derive from the Esmeraldas notes in Burroughs' letter of Early July 1953.

**35-36** "The boat" to "tourist card": lines derive in part from Burroughs' letter of April 30, 1953 and the "Ecuadorian miscellanea" in his letter of June 6, 1953.

**36** "*Guayaquil*" to "final desolation": lines derive from the "Ecuadorian miscellanea" in Burroughs' letter of June 6, 1953.

**36** "La Asia" to "balcony": lines derive from the Esmeraldas notes in Burroughs' letter of Early July 1953.

**36** "Ecuador" to "amenities": lines derive from the "Ecuadorian miscellanea" in Burroughs' letter of June 6, 1953.

**36** "W. Lee": version in *Big Table* is signed "Bill"; it was marked for changing to "W. Lee" in 1963 (see City Lights Editorial Files, Berkeley).

**37** "The bars around" to "such an occurrence": lines derive from Burroughs' letter of May 12, 1953.

**37-38** "Met a boy" to "White Man's Country": lines derive from the notes in Burroughs' letter of Early July 1953.

**38** "South America" to "deviants in U.S.": lines derive from the Peru notes section of Burroughs' letter of July 10, 1953.

**38-39** "Extensive Chinatown" to "does it here": lines derive from Burroughs' letter of May 12, 1953.

**39** "May 23": what follows derives from Burroughs' letter of May 23/24, 1953.

**39** "Enclose a routine I dreamed up": the letter original has "skit" not routine. In earlier editions, until the "routine" was included in the third edition (1988), there was an asterisk at this point directing the reader to a footnote. In the first edition, the note read:

"This is Burroughs' first *routine*, 'Roosevelt After Inauguration.' The form then took on a life of its own, like the talking asshole in *Naked Lunch*; subsequent letters to Ginsberg developed much of the material of that volume. 'Roosevelt After Inauguration' was printed in *Floating Bear No. 9*; the editor, poet Leroi Jones, was arrested for sending this issue through U.S. Government mails; after a year of harassment Jones was vindicated. Copies of a new pirated edition of this *routine* are obtainable from City Lights Books at 50c postpaid."

Note that a sentence, after "vindicated," was struck from the proofs: "British distributors of the present collection declare they dare not purvey this routine, so it is not printed here." (City Lights Editorial Files, Berkeley)

In the second edition, the footnote was the same, except that the final line was cut. In the third edition, the footnote had the same first two sentences, and continued:

" 'Roosevelt After Inauguration' was deleted from the original edition of *The Yage Letters* by the English printers. The routine was first published in *Floating Bear #9* by Leroi Jones. That issue was seized and an obscenity case brought against it when copies were sent to someone in a penal institution. Subsequently the piece appeared in a mimeo edition from Ed Sander's Fuck You Press, and was published with other short essays by City Lights Books in 1979 as *Roosevelt After Inauguration and Other Atrocities.*"

The 1964 Fuck You publication *Roosevelt After Inauguration* included the note: "This routine was bricked out of the City Lights Volume by paranoid printers in England. It was first stomped into print in Floating Bear #9."

**39** "all my experience as a homosexual": in Burroughs' letter of May 24, 1953 he inserted (and then struck through) the word "international" before "homosexual" and then "traveler" after it.

**41** "ROOSEVELT AFTER INAUGURATION": the text was first included in the third edition of *The Yage Letters*, having previously appeared, with minor differences, in: *Floating Bear* No. 9 (June 1961) where it was titled "Routine: Roosevelt after Inauguration"; in pamphlet form published by Fuck You Press in 1964; as "After the Inauguration" in *Notes from Underground* No. 3 (1970); in *Crawdaddy* (March 1977); and in *Roosevelt After Inauguration and Other Atrocities* in 1979. Burroughs' original five page ms. (autograph except for one typed half-page) was enclosed with his letter of May 23, 1953 (GC, CU).

**42** "*Ambassador to the Court of St. James's*": until *Crawdaddy*, all versions of "Roosevelt" had "English Ambassador" here; this was one of several small technical corrections (others included the naming of "Jerk Off Annie" "to the" Joint Chiefs of Staff).

**43** "All right, H.P.": one of very few unused fragments, this line has been restored from the original ms.

**44** "for indecent exposure": this phrase has been restored from the original ms.

**45** "degrade it beyond recognition": although all versions have the same material, from this point on the sequence and paragraphing in Burroughs' ms., in *Floating Bear*, in the Fuck You Press edition, and in *Notes from Underground* differs from that in *Crawdaddy, Roosevelt After Inauguration and Other Atrocities* and *Yage Letters*. The key difference is that in these earlier versions, the final line ("I'll make. . .") originally followed "beyond recognition."

**46** "Comfortable well-run hotel" to "greasy meal": lines derive from the "Tingo María" notes in Burroughs' letter of Early July 1953.

**46** "Stuck here 'til tomorrow" to "I can *see*": lines derive from the "Tingo María" notes in Burroughs' letter of July 8, 1953, except for the line from "The feel of *location*" to "unendurable," which derives from Burroughs' letter of Early July 1953.

**47-48** "Last five days" to "Horribly cold": except for the second paragraph, all this material derives from the "notes" in Burroughs' letter of Early July 1953.

**48** "went over his books": YA has an extra line here; **"(I suspect that when Chinese look enigmatic they are probably engaged in mental book keeping.)"**

**48-49** "Three times" to "leave right now": this material all appears as a block in the ten page tms. enclosed with Burroughs' letter of August 3, 1953 (GC, CU), most of which was used in 1985 to form the "Epilogue" to *Queer*. This material also appears in first draft in the July 16-17 entries of Burroughs' notebook (forthcoming from Ohio State University Press as *"Everything Lost": The Latin American Notebook of William S. Burroughs*).

**49** "from one side of the joint to the other": at this point the August 3, 1953 tms. continues; **"(Like Hunky's** [sic] **senseless furniture moving kicks. Or old paretic Mr. Elvins waking his servant up in the middle of the night to shift all the furniture from one side of the room to the other — )"**

**49** "Love, / Bill": until the third edition, an inverted triangle of asterisks was placed at the center of the page alongside the signing off to mark the end of "In Search of Yage" (i.e., it was retained even after addition of the July 10 letter in the second edition).

**50-52** "Yage is space time travel" to "if they are contagious": this material derives from Burroughs' letter of July 10, 1953. In the following notes, I have given unused phrases from the ms. of this letter (GC, CU) only if they do not appear in *Letters*. With a number of small variations, this material appears at the start of "the market" section of *Naked Lunch*.

**50** "vast weed grown parks": at this point on the letter ms. appears the struck through phrase, **"with benches of rotting stone"**.

**50** "play cryptic games": in the margin of the letter ms. appears a typed inserted phrase; **"Babylonian seals."**

**52** "pus and scabs" to "a disease" and from "These diseased beggars" to "crowded cafe": these lines derive from the "Few additions on diseased beggars in The City" given in Burroughs' letter of July 9, 1953 (see Appendix 2).

**52-53** "Followers of" to "live one": it is not clear when Burroughs first wrote this passage, but he worked on it in 1955 and the earliest ms. of this material is the January 1956 YA.

**53** "A place where the unknown past": *Naked Lunch* (and YA) punctuate these last lines with a significant difference, with ellipses before "A place" and after "hum" and "One".

**57** "June 10, 1960": the first page of Ginsberg's letter (Burroughs-Hardiment Collection, Kansas University) has two marginal comments; **"Save this letter"** and **"My God what have you gone thru, alone."**

**57** "Ramon Penadillo": in previous editions only the first letter of the surname was given.

**59** "There is a branch": omitted in all previous editions, this paragraph has been restored from the manuscript.

**63** "Lucien seemingly an angel": in previous editions, "Simon" was used here as a pseudonym for Lucien Carr; with his death (in 2005), has passed the need to preserve anonymity. Likewise "Francesca" below, replaces "Francine".

**64** "Allen Ginsberg": at this point on the manuscript there appears a vertical marginal comment; **"I.e. I feel trapped in a universe I can't escape from, and don't trust or understand the universe."**

**68** "male and female": this phrase does not appear on the ms., but is on the first edition's long galleys, and was probably an insert made by Ginsberg for publication. These words do appear in the version of "Aether" published in his *Collected Poems* (p. 248).

**69** "O BELL": these lines were not in block caps on the ms. but were marked by Ginsberg for resetting on the long galleys. After the poem, appear these previously untranscribed lines: **"Also felt, that in apocalyptic universe of flying bombs, Something was coming thru to different consciousness from the Central Control."**

**70** "take the enclosed copy": from evidence in the Ginsberg Collection at

Columbia University, Ginsberg did as he was advised, producing a two-page paste up of the block caps material cut into strips and rearranged (although not by quartering the page, but by alternating the lines in a new order).

70 "Brion Gysin": at this point all previous editions had an asterisk directing the reader to the following footnote:

"Brion Gysin: an English painter, collaborator and friend of Burroughs from Tanger, who suggested to him the application of XX Century painter's techniques—the collage—to written composition. *Naked Lunch* was thus finished as a collage of routines. The pamphlets *Minutes to Go* (Two Cities Press, Paris 1960) and *The Exterminator* (Auerhahn Press, San Francisco 1960) were prepared by Gysin, Burroughs, Gregory Corso and others as graphic exposition of an immediate way out of temporal literary and phenomenological hang-ups through collage cut-up techniques.— A.G."

75 "this correspondence": the original draft of this letter (City Lights Collection, Berkeley) had the more narrow phrasing **"this letter"**. The only other significant change between this draft and the published version is the addition of the line, "Old love, as ever".

## Appendix 1

From Burroughs' June 1953 "Yage" manuscript (Ginsberg Papers, Series 1: Correspondence, Box 2 Folder 42, Stanford University).

81 "*Revised in light of subsequent experience*": probably written later in June 1953, these lines are an autograph insert on the margin of the carbon copy of this page.

83 "*Complete tolerance is rapidly acquired. They do not get sick*": again, probably written later in June 1953, these lines are an autograph insert on the margin of the carbon copy of this page.

## Appendix 2

Burroughs' letter to Ginsberg, July 9, 1953 (GC, CU).

84 "July 9, 1953": date and place derived from envelope.

Appendix 3

From Burroughs' December 1953 "Yage" manuscript (Ginsberg Papers, Series 1: Correspondence, Box 2 Folder 42, Stanford University). The pages are numbered 28 and 29, clearly indicating their place in the larger sequence of "Yage."

**86** "*May 24* [1953]/ *Lima*": date and place are an autograph addition.

Appendix 4

From Burroughs' January 1956 "*Yagé* Article" manuscript (BC, CU).

This material forms the opening section of the first draft manuscript of Burroughs' "*Yagé* Article"; these particular pages appear to have been retyped by Burroughs from a still earlier draft. The material overlaps the text of "In Search of Yage" (pp. 15-16).

**88** "*Jan 3, 56 received*": the date is an autograph insert (in Ginsberg's hand); the title is in autograph (Burroughs' hand).
**90** "Jorge Barragán": author of *Apuntamientos recogidos por el ciudadano Colombiano sobre la Maravillosa Planta del yagé* (1928).
**90** "and have experimented with thought transference": these words are an autograph insert on the manuscript (the only one on these pages, apart from the addition of "by Jorge Barragán").

Appendix 5

From Burroughs' March 1956 "*Yagé* Article" manuscript (BC, CU).

**91-93** "Waiting for a train" to "Same old Panama": this material forms the opening section of the manuscript, ending at the point where "In Search of Yage" continues (p. 4).
**91** "he-man *True* magazines": cut from the January 1956 draft at this point was the line, and aside to Ginsberg; **"(This one entitled simply *Gonads* . . . For those that have them. Not sold to women, minors or hermaphrodites . . omit if you think necessary.)"**

**91** "*ayahuasca*": throughout this ms. Burroughs used the idiosyncratic spelling **"Ayuahuaska,"** even though the standard spelling appears in his January 1956 draft.

**93-97** "From Bogotá I flew down to Lima" to "two days in Huánuco": this material appears on pages 15-19 of the 25 page ms. In relation to "In Search of Yage," this sequence effectively appears in between the "fundamental split" of the Colombian Civil War (p. 38) and the description of Huánuco (p. 48).

**94** "You do not feel the influence of Spain in Lima": this line, possibly cut but more likely accidentally omitted from the January 1956 draft, has been restored here, as has the word "pure" in the last line of the paragraph.

**97** "invading my flesh": at this point the January 1956 draft has the extra line; **"I experience convulsions of lust accompanied by physical impotence."**

**97** "*Palicourea Species Rubiaceae*": at this point the January 1956 draft has the extra line; **"The Indian name is Caway."**

**98-100** "*Appendix Summary*": this section follows several pages in the main article that overlap the "July 8" and "July 10" letters of "In Search of Yage." This formed the basis to Burroughs' "Letter from a Master Addict to Dangerous Drugs" for the *British Journal of Addiction* (January 1957). That text in turn became the Appendix to all editions of *Naked Lunch* after the first (which had included the *yagé* part of it — in effect, the "Appendix Summary" of the "*Yagé* Article" — as a long footnote).

**99** "beyond ordinary consciousness": at this point the January 1956 draft has an extra line; **"You glimpse new forms of being."**

Appendix 6

From Ginsberg's June 1960 South American Journal (Ginsberg Papers, Series 2: Notebooks and Journals, Stanford University).

WILLIAM BURROUGHS is recognised as one of the most innovative, politically trenchant, and influential artists of the twentieth century. Born in 1914 into a social register St. Louis family, he became a key figure, along with Jack Kerouac and Allen Ginsberg, in the Beat Generation of writers who emerged in the early 1950s. After leaving America, Burroughs documented his experiences as a heroin addict and a homosexual in *Junky* and *Queer* before achieving international notoriety in 1959 with *Naked Lunch*. Inspired by the artist Brion Gysin, Burroughs then launched his "cut-up" project, which included a trilogy of novels — *The Soft Machine, The Ticket That Exploded, Nova Express* — as well as experiments in tape, film, and photomontage. Having lived in Mexico, South America, North Africa, and finally Europe, in the 1970s Burroughs returned to America, where he settled in Lawrence, Kansas. He completed a final trilogy of novels — *Cities of the Red Night, The Place of Dead Roads, The Western Lands* — as well as collaborating with other artists in several media. He died on August 2, 1997.

OLIVER HARRIS began as a Burroughs scholar with a Ph.D. at Christ Church, Oxford, in the 1980s. Since then he has edited *The Letters of William S. Burroughs, 1945–1959* (1993) and *Junky: the definitive text of "Junk"* (2003), as well as publishing numerous critical articles and the book *William Burroughs and the Secret of Fascination* (2003). Following *The Yage Letters Redux*, he is co-editing *"Everything Lost": The Latin American Notebook of William S. Burroughs.* He is Professor of American Literature at Keele University.